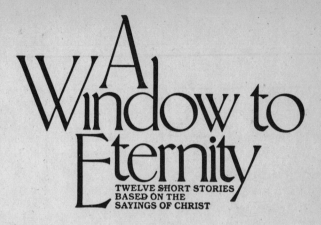

A Window to Eternity

**TWELVE SHORT STORIES
BASED ON THE
SAYINGS OF CHRIST**

ED STEWART

Illustrated by Ted Killian

Regal Books
A Division of GL Publications
Ventura, California, U.S.A.

Rights for publishing this book in other languages are contracted by Gospel Literature International foundation (GLINT). GLINT also provides technical help for the adaptation, translation, and publishing of Bible study resources and books in more than 100 languages worldwide. For further information, contact GLINT, Post Office Box 6688, Ventura, California 93006, U.S.A., or the publisher.

Published by Regal Books
A Division of GL Publications
Ventura, California 93006
Printed in U.S.A.

Library of Congress Cataloging in Publication Data

Stewart, Ed.
    A window to eternity.

    Summary: The theme of each of the twelve stories is introduced by a passage from the New Testament quoting Jesus Christ.
    1. Short stories, American. [1. Christian life—
Fiction. 2. Short stories] I. Title.
PZ7.S84879Wi   1985   [Fic]   85-11739
ISBN 0-8307-1052-3

Dedication

Affectionately dedicated to my co-workers in youth ministry at Evergreen Christian Center, who read and discussed many of these stories in manuscript form with their classes:

Dan and Denise Doyle
Jim and Kim Gilmer
Wendell and Nancy King
Carol Ramey
Carol Shaver

Thanks for appreciating the stories and loving the storyteller!

And special thanks to Carol Stewart—my wife, best friend, and most affirming critic, and to our kids Ken and Kris, in whom I am well pleased.

"Praise and glory and wisdom and thanks and honor and power and strength be to our God for ever and ever. Amen!" (Rev. 7:12, *NIV*)

Contents

A Window to Eternity

"I am the good shepherd. The good shepherd lays down his life for the sheep." John 10:11

The four NASA cadets emerged from their sleeping quarters aboard ARLO-5 long before their 0530 wake-up call from Houston. The celebration of their soon return to the Cape and graduation from the NASA Academy in Houston had kept them awake past 2300 the night before. But the anticipation of their last full day of lab work, culminating one month of "finals" in orbit, had awakened them early.

The cadets hovered in the pod midway between the living quarters and the control module as 20-year-old Cam O'Donnell, the cadet team leader, distributed breakfast packets of granola bars and dried fruit to his 19-year-old subordinates. Cam's quiet confidence and maturity had earned him the respect of his team.

"Not steak and eggs again," quipped Ted Trisk sarcastically as he snatched a packet gliding toward him from Cam's hand. Trisk's humor had provided a welcome counterbalance to the subconscious anxiety which accompanied the cadets' confinement.

"I'll trade you for eggs benedict," responded Nobi Ishika, the petite female member of the team. Nobi and Trisk exchanged identical packets with mock ceremony while Cam and cadet Erik Braddy began munching on granola bars.

"Countdown check," Cam announced, glancing at his chronograph. "In less than 30 hours we will be sitting around a platter of prime rib at Finny's place." Cam's teammates hummed their anticipation.

Dr. Alan Finniman, the project director of academy labs, coached his cadets into the wonders of extraterrestrial science like a mother duck coaxes her young into a pond. After nurturing academy upperclassmen through their final year in Houston and escorting them on at least two brief orbital lab missions, the cadets' beloved Finny sent each qualified group to ARLO-5 alone for their final labs. "You have a month to play in God's backyard," Finny was fond of saying as he tapped each cadet's helmet prior to launch. "I'll have prime rib dinner waiting for you if and when you can tear yourself away from ARLO-5."

The Audio Research Laboratory Operation comprised the most sophisticated listening station of the 14 space labs orbiting Earth. The five pods of the ARLO complex resembled a floating, U-shaped necklace of five giant canisters strung together by a tubular chain catwalk which connected the pods. The two ends of the catwalk, adjacent to pods 1 and 5, served as shuttle docks.

Each cylindrical pod supported an assortment of antennae, dishes, transmitters, and receivers. The tentacles of pods 1-3 stretched toward Earth monitoring global communications. Pods 4 and 5 were originally constructed as deep space "ears"—super sensitive listening labs eagerly straining to receive the slightest attempts at communication from galaxies beyond. But after several silent decades, ARLO-4 was scaled down to an automated deep space probe relay station. And ARLO-5 was converted into a NASA Academy lab for upperclassmen who were being groomed for positions in NASA's elite technical corps.

When they had stowed their refuse from breakfast, the four cadets, clad in their powder blue jumpsuits, hand-walked their weightless forms to the hatch of the control module. They entered single-file and strapped into place in front of four computer terminals.

Cam quickly reviewed for his team the final phase of their current project: locate the unmanned NASA Venus Probe 6, lock into its memory, and evaluate data regarding atmospheric conditions, soil content, and life forms. Then the team leader contacted Houston and supplied ARLO Control with their agenda. Braddy retrieved location data for VP-6 and Trisk punched in the coordinates to manipulate the pod's giant dish. Nobi awaited the first items of atmospheric data for analysis.

"Heavy interference today," Nobi wrinkled her tiny nose as a steady *whish* of static poured from the module's speaker. "I'm not getting any response signals from the probe."

"The monitor tells me we're locked onto VP-6," Cam reported, "but I'm getting no video display and no audio signal—just this heavy fuzz."

"Our last day to play in God's backyard and we end up sitting through a sandstorm in a tin shed," Trisk muttered as he instructed the computer to mute the interference. The hiss on the speaker diminished slightly.

"I'm picking up something behind the fuzz," Braddy cocked his ear toward the speaker. "But it doesn't sound like an electronic signal."

"Still negative on the video display," Cam announced.

The cadets sat motionless and breathless to listen.

"Incredible! It sounds like music!" Braddy almost whined in disbelief. "It's like a stadium full of people chanting or singing!"

"That's impossible!" Nobi exclaimed. "This is an audio hookup to an electronic frequency, not a stereo amplifier."

Again the pod was silent except for a mysterious, haunting chant bleeding through a blanket of interference. "It must be a satellite skip or an echo from another lab," Nobi offered, realizing that she was illogically grasping for a logical explanation.

"It's too deep for a skip," Trisk stated the obvious. "I think it's the Houston Symphony. I always thought their music was far out." For once Trisk's attempt at humor was hollow, and provoked more anxiety than relief.

The four cadets lapsed into another two minutes of silent listening, struggling to remain analytical and scientific in the face of an unexplainable phenomenon which poked at their sleeping fears of the unknowns of fathomless space.

"I'm picking up a pattern," Braddy's expression reflected the intensity of his interest. "The chanty-like tune repeats every minute or so, but the syllables change like each cycle is a different verse of the song."

"Or each cycle is the same verse in another language," Nobi advanced.

Cam jumped ahead of the conversation and began stroking the keyboard of his terminal. Trisk, Braddy, and Nobi immediately keyed their monitors to Cam's terminal as the words "INTERNATIONAL LINGUISTICS" appeared in orange characters. A menu of international linguistic services appeared and Cam scrolled the list until he found what he wanted: "LANGUAGE IDENTIFICA-TION-AUDIO: LINGUISTICS UNLIMITED, LONDON" followed by a series of access digits.

"It seems to be fading," Nobi reported with alarm. The three men strained to listen and agreed.

"Braddy, package what we have heard so far and prepare to transmit," Cam instructed. "Nobi, access the Linguistics Unlimited code in London. Trisk, see if you can nail down a location on this stuff."

"This *cannot* be happening," Trisk almost shouted as he slammed his fist on the console, echoing the fear and frustration they all shared. "We *cannot* receive choir music on instruments designed for electronic signals! I feel like I'm playing *Name That Tune* on the set of *Star Wars*."

Cam's response was firm and controlled. "We can either sit here disbelieving our experience or we can attack it scientifically as we were trained." After a thoughtful moment Trisk sighed his agreement and the cadets turned back to their terminals.

In the few minutes it took to beam the disk's contents to London the music faded obscurely behind the audio haze. Suddenly the response from London began marching across the four screens. The cadets pulled closer to their monitors and read.

SAMPLE 1

KNOWN LANGUAGE
LANGUAGE GROUP: NORTH AMERICAN MINOR EXTINCT
DIALECT: IROQUOIAN CIRCA A.D. 1645-1900
TEXT IN ENGLISH: INFINITE VALUE, THE BUTCHERED LAMB TO THE LAMB BELONGS ALL POWER

AND ALL WEALTH
ALL WISDOM AND ALL
STRENGTH
ALL HONOR AND ALL
GLORY AND ALL PRAISE

SAMPLE 2   KNOWN LANGUAGE
LANGUAGE GROUP: SEMITIC MINOR EXTINCT
DIALECT: ARABIAN REMOTE
                          CIRCA 2300-2000 B.C.
TEXT IN ENGLISH: INFINITE VALUE, THE
                          BUTCHERED LAMB
                          TO THE LAMB BELONGS
                          ALL POWER AND ALL
                          WEALTH
                          ALL WISDOM AND ALL
                          STRENGTH
                          ALL HONOR AND ALL
                          GLORY AND ALL PRAISE

SAMPLE 3   KNOWN LANGUAGE
LANGUAGE GROUP: SCANDINAVIAN MAJOR
                          EXTANT
DIALECT: NORWEGIAN
TEXT IN ENGLISH: INFINITE VALUE, THE
                          BUTCHERED LAMB
                          TO THE LAMB BELONGS
                          ALL POWER AND ALL
                          WEALTH
                          ALL WISDOM AND ALL
                          STRENGTH
                          ALL HONOR AND ALL
                          GLORY AND ALL PRAISE

Two more complete samples appeared identifying obscure dialects from Chinese and Ukrainian language groups. But the text in English was the same—a eulogy to a slain lamb to whom was ascribed ownership of seven universal values.

The cadets sat in perplexed silence, each one processing the data from the report through a wide range of hidden feelings and fears.

"Location, Trisk?" Cam asked softly.

"It's beyond our hardware," Trisk almost whispered. "The computer recognizes a valid transmission but answers all my questions with the same word—'UNKNOWN.'"

"Maybe NASA shut down the deep space 'ears' too soon," Nobi wondered aloud.

Suddenly Braddy swung toward his keyboard and started tapping instructions furiously. "I may be wrong," he said as his fingers danced across the keys, "but that 'butchered lamb' stuff sounds like biblical jargon. I have an aunt in Seattle who's a religious nut. She's crammed her IBQ 9690 with reams of biblical data."

"You mean there's a planet out there full of people singing Bible verses?" Trisk pushed sarcastically. His teammates did not answer but turned again to their monitors as the Seattle-based IBQ 9690 granted Braddy access. He instructed the computer to perform a related data search and then carefully typed in the words, "INFINITE VALUE, THE BUTCHERED LAMB."

"Does your aunt mind if you tamper with her files?" Nobi asked Braddy as he punched "ENTER."

"If you only knew how many times Aunt Beth has bugged me to examine some of her biblical data," Braddy answered with a forced chuckle. "When she finds out I have accessed her biblical files from orbit she'll probably think she's died and gone to heav . . . " Braddy was afraid to voice the surprising thoughts which had just entered his mind. *Heaven?* he thought. *Music from heaven? Angelic choirs in deep space?*

"Remember how Finny talks about 'playing in God's backyard'?" Nobi's tentative question paralleled Braddy's radical thought. "Maybe—somehow—we just wandered by His open window."

Nobi's hypothesis was punctuated by a spray of orange characters illuminating the four monitors—the IBQ 9690's reply. Each cadet turned toward a monitor as line after line of data danced across the screen under the heading:

"RELATED DATA: INFINITE VALUE, THE BUTCH-ERED LAMB."

The report began with numerous excerpts from Judeo-biblical writings citing the development of the Hebraic system of animal sacrifices. Goats, bulls, and especially lambs were periodically offered by the Hebrews to their God as an atonement for their shortcomings.

After a break in the text the report continued with segments from Christo-biblical inscriptions, principally the writings of Saint John the Apostle. "Look, the Lamb of God who takes away the world's sin!" Cam read one line softly under his breath. Then he mouthed another curious saying ascribed to Christ and recorded by Saint John: "I am the good shepherd. The good shepherd lays down his life for the sheep."

The third section of data concerned the futuristic writings of Saint John. "Look!" Nobi gasped as she pointed to the final paragraph on her monitor. Each cadet's eyes widened in wonder as they read the concluding lines of the report: "I looked and heard the voice of many angels, numbering thousands upon thousands, and ten thousand times ten thousand. In a loud voice they sang: 'Infinite value, the butchered lamb. To the lamb belongs all power and all wealth, all wisdom and all strength, all honor and all glory and all praise.'"

The computer clicked the words "END REPORT" and then the pod was quiet except for the soft *whish* of oxygen circulating through ARLO-5. Finally Cam assumed command and spoke softly, "I think we are in over our heads. I'd like to call Finny if no one objects." His partners nodded.

In less than a minute Cam had raised Houston and obtained a security patch through to Dr. Finniman at the Cape. "ARLO-5, this is Finniman. Good morning, team!" Finny's voice echoed his warmth and good nature.

"Good morning, Dr. Finniman," Cam tried to sound cordial and unruffled. "We've run into something we need to talk to you about right away, sir." He felt no alternative but to get right to the point. "We were trying to contact Venus 6 this morning and picked up something we can't identify. It was a vocal communication, like a thousand voices singing. We cannot locate a source and we don't know . . . "

"So you've heard the music, have you?" Dr. Finniman's voice was low and soft but full of empathy.

"Why, yes sir!" Cam responded with surprise. "How did you know?"

Finny did not answer Cam's question, but instead began humming the familiar, penetrating melody the cadets had detected on their instruments only minutes earlier. "How do you know that tune, sir?" Braddy interrupted.

"I first heard the song almost 30 years ago while interning aboard ARLO-4. I couldn't understand it either. My superiors dismissed it as a satellite skip, but my guts would not let me excuse it so lightly. So I started listening for it. I heard it again at least three times from ARLO-4—once in French—and began to understand its meaning.

Since then I've heard it in a roaring waterfall in the Rockies, in a howling storm on the Cape, and in the blast of an Orion rocket."

"Why didn't you tell us about it?" Trisk insisted loudly.

"Would you have believed me?" Dr. Finniman's question brought Trisk up short. The cadets were having difficulty believing their *own* experience.

"What does it mean, sir?" Nobi framed the question which was chewing at the core of their scientific minds.

"Even the little I know would take more than a lifetime to explain, Nobi," Dr. Finniman answered with a sigh. "But my advice to you is simple: listen for it, learn it. It's a universal, eternal anthem celebrating the Great Shepherd who died as a sacrificial lamb so that the rest of us, his wayward sheep, might live."

Suddenly Cam jerked toward the speaker. "It's coming through again!" he cried.

Cam and his team responded almost automatically. They slipped out of their chairs and guided their weightless bodies toward the floor of the module until their knees touched. Then with Dr. Finniman and the unseen choir they began singing to the lamb.

Thought Questions

1. What strange sound did the crew of ARLO-5 hear? Why was it interpreted as being sung in so many languages, some of which were extinct?

2. What was the message? What was its purpose?

3. What things do worldly shepherds do for their flocks? How can this be compared to what Jesus does for His flock?

4. Jesus is the Good Shepherd who cares for His sheep. The Bible says His sheep will recognize His voice (John 10:4,14). How do people hear Jesus' voice in the world today?

Stumbling into the Light

"Jesus said to her, 'I am the resurrection and the life. He who believes in me will live, even though he dies; and whoever lives and believes in me will never die. Do you believe this?'" John 11:25, 26

Jorim crept through the dark streets of Bethany as quietly as a cat. The 16-year-old's dark features and brown wool tunic merged him with the shadows as he approached the back wall of the tax collector's house. He leaped effortlessly and grasped the ledge of the elevated back window of the house. His powerful arms pulled him upward while his bare feet scaled the clay brick wall. While perched on the window ledge, he slid the blade of his knife between the shutters and released the latch. Then he slowly pushed the shutters open.

The boy slithered soundlessly down the inside wall of the house and then froze in the pitch blackness to listen.

He heard only the muted howl of a stray dog somewhere on Mount Olivet and the raspy, measured breathing of the tax collector to his left inside the large, one room structure. Excitement mingled with fear shot through Jorim's veins as he plotted his next move.

The small, slender youth felt his way along the wall farthest from the sleeping tax collector until he reached the front door. He carefully lifted the bolting beam and laid it on the floor against the wall, clearing the path for a quick escape.

The money box should be on the floor next to the bed, Jorim reminded himself as he lowered to his knees and began crawling in the direction of the heavy snoring. Once he had eased himself around a large, oak table, Jorim could see the faint outline of the tax collector's huge frame turned toward the wall. The dark image of a large box appeared on the floor a few inches from the old man's head. The young thief inched his way toward the box and slowly lifted the lid.

Crash! A clay goblet on top of the money box slid to the brick floor and shattered. The old man gasped and snorted as he jerked upright in bed. "Who's there?" he bellowed.

Jorim sprang to his feet and lunged in the direction of the door, only to crash into the table, sending two more goblets and a plate clattering to the floor. Glancing off the table, he stumbled over a stool and fell backwards to the floor with a groan. The boy's eyes, wide with terror, clearly saw the old man rise, grab a wooden staff from beside the bed, and stagger toward him, cursing loudly. The staff whooped through the air, smacking the corner of the table and dislodging another plate. Jorim scrambled between the legs of the table and lurched toward the door as the old man assaulted the table again with another wild swing.

Jorim was out the door and racing up the Street of Palms before the staff landed again. "Stop the thief!" Jorim heard the tax collector shout as he sprinted through the deserted streets which were lightly dusted with starlight. He ran through the marketplace, past the well in the square, and up a narrow alleyway until the sounds of disturbance were well behind him. He slowed to a trot, panting heavily and favoring his right foot with every shortening stride. The adrenalin which had masked the pain during the flight suddenly drained away and Jorim hobbled to a low wall, sat down, and reached for his foot.

The boy gasped at the shock of pain as he touched the badly scraped and rapidly swelling top of his right foot. His memory replayed his escape from the tax collector's house and the panic-filled stride toward the door which sent his right foot slamming into the table leg with full force.

Still fearing pursuit by the old man, Jorim limped awkwardly to the top of the alleyway and through a small olive orchard to the wall bordering the courtyard of his uncle's home. He slid quietly over the wall and limped heavily up the outside stairway to the roof where his cot was waiting under a canvas tent. He collapsed on his cot and moaned as his swollen foot brushed against the wool blanket.

Jorim suddenly felt lonely in the darkness. He cursed the predicament which had exiled him to the house in Bethany his uncle Lazarus shared with two widowed sisters, Mary and Martha. Only two years ago Jorim lived with his parents in Jerusalem where the boy had secretly joined a gang of young burglars. But within a four-month period both of Jorim's parents died and Lazarus responsibly assumed guardianship of his nephew, moving the boy from Jerusalem to his home in Bethany.

Lazarus is a good man, Jorim thought as he squirmed on his cot trying to elevate his aching foot on a pillow. *And he is a good pharmacist too.* As a maker of potions, poultices, and perfumes, Lazarus had dutifully begun training his nephew in his craft. But Jorim had already selected a trade—one which often produced a much more lucrative return in the hours after midnight than the boy had realized tonight. How he longed to be back in the streets of Jerusalem, but somehow he was unable to abandon the goodness he found in his uncle and aunts.

"Jorim!" Martha's call awakened the boy as morning sunlight illumined the eastern side of his tent. There was a trace of panic in his aunt's voice. Jorim's heart jumped into his throat as he imagined the tax collector waiting for him at the base of the stairs.

"Jorim! Please come down quickly! Lazarus is very ill! I cannot awaken him!" Martha was beginning to weep. Jorim's stomach instantly knotted with fear as he sensed the loss of another loved one. *Not him, Lord,* the boy muttered under his breath. *Take a clumsy cat burglar instead of a godly pharmacist.* The boy was surprised by his own thoughts.

Jorim's first step from the cot was extremely painful and he nearly collapsed. His right foot was greatly swollen and discolored. He limped slowly down the stairs and into the house where his two aunts stood beside Lazarus' bed. His uncle's face was pasty white and his breathing was shallow. "The mask of death," Lazarus had termed the symptomatic pallor when Jorim had accompanied him to the homes of the incurably ill.

"What can I do?" Jorim asked, feeling helpless. "I don't know the prescriptions."

"He is beyond our help," Mary said quietly. "Jorim, you must go at once and find the Master and tell Him about Lazarus."

The Master? Jorim mused. *How could a young carpenter-turned rabbi help a man who obviously has an appointment with death?*

Jesus had been in Lazarus' home many times since Jorim had arrived. The young rabbi's visits had been accompanied by raucous crowds straining and shoving to hear Him speak or to touch His hand. Jorim avoided Jesus and His followers by retreating to the roof, the orchard, or the solitude of Olivet's summit when the throngs began to gather. Only once had Jorim exchanged greetings with Jesus, and that quite by surprise. Jorim was sneaking back to his rooftop bed one pre-dawn morning only to find the Master standing on the roof, arms outstretched toward the heavens praying. Jorim had tiptoed halfway across the roof when Jesus suddenly dropped His arms and turned toward the boy.

"Good morning," He said with a warmth which matched the soft glow looming on the eastern horizon.

"G-g-good morning," Jorim responded nervously, then disappeared into his tent. Thereafter Jorim slept in the stable during Jesus' visits, even though he was strangely attracted to the warmth of his uncle's teacher and friend.

"Where am I to find Him and what shall I say?" Jorim asked his aunt, at once both fearful of an encounter with the Master and desirous of drawing near to His warmth.

"He is teaching beyond the Jordan, just north of the ford opposite Jericho," Mary informed. "You will see the crowds there and they will direct you to Him." Mary picked up a small, polished onyx box and placed it in Jorim's hand. "When you find the Master, tell Him that the maker of this ointment, His dearly beloved friend, is at the point of death."

"How will He know me?" Jorim doubted that Jesus would remember their chance meeting on the rooftop.

"He will recognize the ointment," Mary assured. "It is His favorite fragrance."

Within an hour Jorim was astride the family donkey riding out of Bethany on the road to Jericho. He had a woolen cloak, a water skin, and a cloth bag containing figs, nuts, and honey cakes which Martha had prepared for him. The box of ointment was stuffed inside Jorim's purse which he carried in the folds of his tunic.

By early afternoon Jorim reached Jericho. After a brief rest in a sycamore grove, the boy pushed steadily on to the west Jordan, arriving shortly before sundown. The view from the ridge above the Jordan Valley revealed numerous spirals of smoke arising from the campfires of a large company of people.

Once across the river, Jorim's inquiries about the Master's camp led him through scores of noisy campsites to an area at the base of a grassy hill dotted with oaks. As Jorim tethered his donkey with some other animals and limped painfully toward the site, a group of Jesus' followers were dispersing a large crowd of seekers to their own campfires. The boy gingerly threaded his way through the crowd and approached one of the disciples.

"Pardon me, sir," Jorim addressed the disciple respectfully. "I have just arrived from Bethany with an important message for the Master from the sisters of His beloved friend Lazarus."

"Well," the disciple answered, "I have been to Bethany many times and have lodged with brother Lazarus." Jorim detected that the disciple was looking for some proof of his claim.

"I am Jorim, a nephew who now lives with Lazarus as a son." The disciple nodded approvingly. "My aunt Mary sends this gift to the Master"—Jorim pulled the box of ointment from his tunic—"with the urgent request that He come to Bethany at once. The Master's beloved friend Lazarus is ill to the point of death."

"Lazarus? Ill?" the disciple raised his brows in surprise, receiving the box. "Yes, the Master must know immediately." He turned in the direction of a small tent spread under a giant oak. After two steps the disciple stopped and faced Jorim again. "Welcome to our camp, Jorim," the disciple smiled. "I am John Bar-Zebedee. You will eat and sleep with us tonight." John gestured toward a heap of glowing coals where four other men were preparing to broil some fish. Jorim nodded his thanks as John again turned toward the tent. The boy retrieved his bundle from the donkey, hobbled to the fire, and found an inconspicuous place to spread his cloak.

"The Master is saddened by the news of Lazarus' illness," John announced as the group of men ate by the fire. "But He declares that the sickness will not end in death." Several men responded by saying, "Hallelujah," but Jorim was astonished by John's statement, *I have seen the mask of death on numbers of Lazarus' patients,* Jorim thought frantically, *and every one of them died!* He doubted that the Master would make a good pharmacist and wondered why such a popular teacher would make such a ridiculous statement. *Worst of all, His followers believe Him!* Jorim shook his head silently in the firelight.

Jesus was exhausted, John had said, and had retired for the night. Jorim kept respectfully silent as the disciples returned to their conversation about the day's events. The boy could not believe that, even if the Master returned to Bethany tonight, Lazarus' destiny could be affected. But he had delivered the message and now sat within a few yards of a source of warmth which attracted him like a magnet.

Shortly after dark the noisy valley quieted to gentle laughter and soft lullabyes as the population bedded down for the night. Jorim turned restlessly in his cloak, pained by his throbbing foot and probed by disquieting questions: *Who is this man who foolishly says the dying will not die, yet warms me like a beckoning campfire? Why does He have such a large and loyal following? And why would such a popular figure interrupt His rooftop prayers to wish a young thief good morning?* Finally, waves of journey weariness overtook the boy and submerged him in sleep.

Jorim was not prepared for the sight which greeted him the next morning. Hundreds of chattering, singing people were tramping by his campsite as he opened his eyes. They were marching up the hillside to a grassy clearing high on Jordan's east bank. Jorim rolled quickly from his cloak, grabbed two figs from his bag, and began hopping and limping curiously up the hillside with the crowd.

Most of the crowd sat on the sun-sprayed grass surrounding a low stump where Jesus sat. Jorim selected a low-hanging branch of a sprawling oak where he could rest his back on the trunk, elevate his foot, and hide in the shadows. There from his perch on that brilliant morning— a time when he was usually sleeping—Jorim watched a day of beauty unfold before him.

The Master spoke simple but powerful words about walking in the light of God's presence and glory, and shunning the deeds of darkness. He gathered children in His arms, nuzzling them and making them laugh. Then He blessed them. He touched the sick who came to Him and they were restored to health. "That man was crippled and now he is walking!" Jorim sat up and blurted out loud as a wave of applause and praise rippled across the hillside. Jorim found himself singing with the crowd psalms of praise which before he had only listened to his family sing. The glorious scene before him warmed him more than the friendly sunlight filtering through the branches above him and reminded him of the glow of a special summer morning on the rooftop. Jorim silently begged the sun not to set today.

That night Jesus sat with the disciples for the evening meal and Jorim was wide-eyed with delight. "We're going back to Judea tomorrow so I can minister to our friend

Lazarus," He announced. Part of Jorim wanted to argue that Lazarus was certainly dead by now, but a slightly larger part of him somehow knew that the Master could minister to Lazarus whether he was alive or dead. The thought burned in Jorim's soul and excited him.

The disciples resisted Jesus' plan by citing previous violence by those who opposed the Master. Jesus quieted their argument with an upraised hand. "A man who walks by day will not stumble, for he sees by this world's light," He said firmly. Then He looked Jorim square in the eyes as He continued, "It is when he walks by night that he stumbles, for he has no light."

Jorim gulped so loudly that he thought everyone around the fire could hear him. The Master's gaze was as warm as ever, but His words were like ice in Jorim's heart. *Night? Darkness? Stumble?* Jorim screamed inside. *He knows that I'm a thief! He knows about my night raids in Bethany! He knows that I hurt my foot by stumbling in the tax collector's house!*

"You have taught us well concerning the Kingdom of God being full of light and the Kingdom of the Evil One being full of darkness," John spoke up, interrupting Jorim's frantic thoughts. "You are saying then that our return to Judea to minister will succeed in spite of the opposition because we walk in the light of obedience."

"And those who oppose God's kingdom will ultimately fail," added another disciple across the fire from Jorim, "just as surely as someone walking in the darkness will stumble."

Jesus nodded with a confident smile, then turned again to Jorim. "So then where should a man walk?" Jesus was as surely calling for Jorim's response as if the hillside were deserted except for the two of them.

Jorim could feel the warmth pour into his eyes through Jesus' gaze. "In-in th-the light of God's kingdom and n-not in the darkness," Jorim stammered just above a whisper. Jesus smiled broadly and nodded. Jorim suddenly knew that he would no more be the same after tonight than a dark room is the same after it is penetrated by a brilliant torch. With a sigh of relief, Jorim shrouded himself with his cloak, curled up by the fire, and fell asleep.

Jorim was startled to find the sky very dark when he awakened. The disciples were still breathing heavily as the faint light of morning crept into the eastern horizon. Jorim saw the shadows near the top of the hill move. A figure was standing against the eastern sky. It was Jesus and He was praying.

Quickly and quietly Jorim was on his feet. The stinging pain in his foot slowed him only slightly as he stepped silently between the sleeping disciples and began his purposeful ascent of the hill.

He paused as he approached the silhouette of the Master facing the wispy pink horizon. "Good morning," Jorim called. Jesus turned immediately to face him.

"Good morning to you, Jorim," He returned, walking down the hill until He was within arm's reach of the boy.

"Please excuse me for interrupting your prayers, Master," Jorim began slowly. Then he blurted out his entire story—the death of his parents, his move to Bethany, his nighttime burglaries, and the incident at the tax collector's house when he injured his foot. The more he spoke, the brighter loomed the sky behind the Master. It was as if dawn was breaking within his soul after a lifetime of darkness.

"I don't want to walk in the darkness anymore," Jorim concluded. "I want to be a man who walks in the light like Lazarus, Mary, Martha—and you." Jesus spread open His arms with a chuckle and Jorim leaped into them. He felt warmer than he had ever felt as he rested in the Master's arms. Then he realized that Jesus was praying over him and blessing him, just as He had done to the children.

Jesus wrapped His arm around Jorim's shoulder as the two began walking down the hill toward the fire which the disciples were building.

"Don't worry about Lazarus," Jesus instructed. "He will be all right."

"Yes, Master, I know," the boy answered.

Suddenly Jorim stopped. He had taken several steps down the hillside before he realized that he wasn't limping.

Thought Questions

1. Christ returned to Bethany to raise Lazarus from the dead (see John 11:25,26,43,44). In what areas of his life did Jorim also experience Christ's renewing power?

2. Christ can restore dead relationships, revive dead youth groups, and revitalize our personal relations with God the Father. Describe one or more such experiences in your own life.

3. List the areas of your life that still need a touch of Christ's renewing power.

The Epistles of Angela Tibbs

"Make every effort to enter through the narrow door, because many, I tell you, will try to enter and will not be able to." Luke 13:24

Monday, July 15, 11:17 A.M.

Dear Stacy,

Well, here I am on my way to Senior High Summer Camp at Silver Lake (remember when we used to call it Sliver Lake from riding the logs?). Do you realize this is the first summer in four years we haven't gone to camp together??? And this is our freshman year—our first year in the *BIG TIME*!!! I don't understand why your parents would ground you for a little thing like borrowing the car without their permission. I guess you should have waited till you got a license. But still, keeping a kid from church camp is almost heathenish!!! I mean REALLY!!!

I hope you can read this, as I am riding in the church bus and we are sitting three to a seat. We are all crowded in the front of the bus because Wendell Boggs is throwing up in the back of the bus. He was bragging about the huge breakfast he had—bacon and zucchini omelette, grapefruit juice, and six slices of raisin nut toast. Then YUK!!! If you think a bacon and zucchini omelette looks gross *before* you eat it—I can't bring myself to finish this sentence!!! Mr. Bigby, our bus driver, says we're stopping for lunch at Taco Macho. At least the aroma in the bus will be different for the afternoon drive.

Just like we planned, I'm bringing almost 200 jumbo packs of bubble gum to sell at camp. What a *GREAT* idea!!! Especially since the Kavity Kabin doesn't sell any gum at all!!! I'm going to split the profits with you since you helped buy the gum. TOGETHER FOREVER!!! I've got it all hidden in my suitcase, overnight case, and even some stuffed into my sleeping bag. I'm keeping it hidden so I won't be a stumbling block to the staff, even though I've never seen a rule that says "NO GUM IN CAMP." Rusty Orr, the youth pastor, was sniffing my luggage while he was loading it onto the bus. He asked me if I bought my cologne at Baskin-Robbins. I REALLY cracked up!!!

Camp is going to be so neat!!! *I AM SERIOUS!!!* I'm praying that Darin Keller gets saved this year because he is SO CUTE and I think he likes me. REALLY!!!

Well, I see Taco Macho ahead on the highway so I'd better close for now. Wendell is feeling better—I just hope he doesn't order any zucchini tacos. HA!!!

Love ya',
Angie

Tuesday, July 16, 8:37 A.M.

Dear Stacy,

I'm writing this letter during my morning devotions because I have a VERY SPECIAL *UNSPOKEN* REQUEST for you to pray about!!! I AM *SERIOUS*!!! Last night during the opening session, Reverend Stutzman (he's the district superintendent and camp dean, remember?) was reading off the camp rules. There were the same ones we always have—no food fights, no pinecone throwing, no pairing off after dark (I looked at Darin after that one but he was looking at Briget Belcher). Then he read a NEW one!!! Can you guess what it was??? *NO GUM IN CAMP!!!* Really!!! I couldn't believe my ears!!! Tina Osgood, who was sitting beside me, had just bought two packs of grape and nearly choked on the first piece. And three guys from cabin 21 (the guys who always build pyramids out of empty milk cartons) demanded a refund after the meeting—and they each bought five packs!!! What a totally DUMB rule!!!

So pray that the Lord will change Reverend Stutzman's mind about this DUMB rule. And pray that the Lord will help the kids in camp to know what to do (especially the kids who brought lots of money!!!). And especially pray that somebody develops a taste for peanut butter flavor—it's not going too good!!!

Since there's not enough time left to read my Bible verses I'll tell you the rest of the news. There are 12 girls in our cabin—six from Central on the other side of the bathroom, and six of us from Community on this side. I'm sleeping in the bunk above Brenda Spielmier—she snores like a rusty chain saw. I AM SERIOUS!!!

Our counselor is Maxine Upshaw from Central. She's okay for an older lady (she's almost 35!!!) and she didn't complain too much about the layer of Vaseline we spread on the toilet seat this morning.

There's the bell—I gotta go to missions class. Our speaker is a missionary to India. BORRRRING!!! Pray for me!!! Pray for Darin!!! Pray for Darin and me (do you know what I mean???) Do NOT pray for Briget Belcher!!!

Toodles,
Angie

Wednesday, July 17, 10:25 P.M.

Dear Stacy,

WHAT AN ANSWER TO PRAYER!!! I'm sitting in morning class right now listening to Pastor Ghormley from the Twin Creeks Church. Do you know what he just said??? Us Christians are supposed to be good stewards of our time, talent, and treasure. Being wasteful is a sin!!! Do you know what that MEANS??? God is telling me to use my *TALENT* for selling bubble gum during my free *TIME* so I can increase my *TREASURE* and give more to Him. I'm thinking about tithing five percent of my share of the profits to the missionary. He's collecting an offering this week to start a seminary in New Delly (or is it New Deli???). Do you want me to put your offering in too???

I hope Reverend Stutzman sees the light soon and changes the rule. That way the kids might buy more and I can give more. Praise the Lord!!! Even if he doesn't change the rule, the Bible says we should obey God rather than men!!! REALLY!!! I'm going to keep selling gum until *GOD* tells me to stop!!!

I would have written you during devotions but the staff is starting to search luggage for gum, so I had to spend my devotions time stuffing 141 packs into my mattress through a small hole in the side. Reverend Stutzman announced the search at breakfast this morning after somebody hoisted a pair of Wendell Boggs's boxer shorts up the flagpole with a piece of used bubble gum stuck to every polka dot. Wouldn't you like to see that on film at 11!!!

OTHER NEWS: Rhonda Twitchell got so blessed playing the third verse of "Wonderful Grace of Jesus" on the piano last night during singspiration that her granny glasses slipped off her nose onto the floor. We had to sing the last chorus acapulco while she crawled around on the floor looking for her specs. What a crack-up!!! The boys in cabin 6 declared a hunger strike at breakfast this morning until the cooks bring out some other boxed cereal beside bran flakes with prune. And today is the second day of team competition. Darin Keller's team, the Mighty Slugs, are in the lead. Our team has a chance to catch the Slugs today if Wendell Boggs can beat Darin in the ping pong tournament (DO YOU BELIEVE IN MIRACLES???).

Pastor Ghormley is now closing in prayer so I've gotta go. You can now stop praying for Darin. He and Briget are going together. I AM SERIOUS!!! Just pray for good sales!!!

See you here, there, or in the air,
Angie

Thursday, July 18, 3:08 P.M.

Dear Stacy,

I'm writing to you during the team competition finals mainly because my team, the Fighting Aardvarks, are not in the finals!!! We moved ahead of the other teams yesterday when Wendell Boggs beat Darin Keller in the ping pong tournament (can you BELIEVE IT???). Wendell said his dad has played ping pong with him since he was five years old to develop his hand-and-eye coordination. Now if his dad could only coordinate the rest of him!!! I mean REALLY!!! Wendell also gave credit for his victory to his polka dot shorts still splattered with bubble gum. He said he wore them for good luck.

But the Aardvarks lost a chance to be in the finals this afternoon when Wendell was disqualified during the burp-off. It seems that the ginger ale they were drinking and burping brought up some bad memories for Wendell from the zucchini and rice casserole we had for lunch. YUK!!!

GOOD NEWS!!! Bubble gum sales are up 20 percent today, especially the new flavors like kumquat and cream of tomato. Even some of the seniors are regular customers. But the staff is getting REAL upset because wads of gum and pieces of wrapper are showing up everywhere!!! There are at least five chunks of used gum stuck under every chair in camp. Rhonda Twitchell found a lump of already-chewed peppermint gum in her bowl of corn chowder at dinner last night. And Briget Belcher sat on a chunk of freshly spit out raspberry and now has a big red splotch decorating her best jeans. TOO BAD!!!

Since the staff is now checking pockets and purses regularly, I've had to go UNDERGROUND to keep up with the demand. Last night I took an old hymnal from the chapel back to my cabin. I cut a large hole between "Gladly The Cross I'd Bear" and "O Little Town of Bethlehem" so I can carry six jumbo packs inside the hymnal. Then I took my leather Bible cover off my Bible and put it on the hymnal. The staff thinks I'm the most spiritual freshman they've ever seen since I carry my "Bible" everywhere!!!

Last night at Victory Circle Reverend Stutzman gave us the old "if-the-guilty-party-supplying-the-bubble-gum-will-come-and-confess-to-me-there-will-be-no-punishment" speech. But I just sat there with my leather covered hymnal feeling like a Bible smuggler in Russia. Maybe God is calling me into undercover missionary work and this is my training!!! I mean REALLY!!!

GREAT NEWS!!! Brenda Spielmier just told me that Darin and Briget broke up. She also needs a pack of banana flavor so I've got to go to the cabin. Then Brenda and I are going to watch Darin in the broom hockey finals. Keep PRAYING!!!

Chow,
Angie

P.S.: Do you think Bible smugglers wonder if they are REALLY doing the right thing?

Friday, July 19, 11:00 P.M.

Dear Stacy,

Today might have been the WORST day of my life if it hadn't turned out to be the BEST day of my life. REALLY!!! I'll probably tell you all this in person before this letter reaches you by mail, but I must finish our week-long talk this way.

It all started like every other day in camp: shaving cream fights in the boys' cabins and toothpaste fights in the girls' cabins. A pair of Rusty Orr's fashion briefs went up the flagpole, so at breakfast Rusty read several letters from the camp mailbag—including one from Mrs. Keller reminding Darin to eat his vegetables!!!

Then Reverend Stutzman was called up to open a letter addressed to him. When he opened the envelope we couldn't tell what was in it. He just stared at the letter for a long time without saying anything, but you could tell he wasn't very happy with what he saw. Then all the laughing and talking stopped and everyone just stared at him with his eyes glued to his letter. After a couple of minutes he opened his mouth to talk and BROKE DOWN CRYING!!! We found out later that the "letter" was a copy of the camp rules with a four-letter word spelled out across it in letters made with flattened pieces of bubble gum.

Reverend Stutzman covered his face until he gained control of himself. Then all he said was, "If you only knew what you were doing," and dismissed us to Pastor Ghormley's last class. There wasn't a sound as we walked from the dining hall to the chapel. I didn't know yet what the "letter" said, but I had a stabbing feeling that Reverend Stutzman's one-sentence sermon was for me. When we got to the chapel nobody would sit next to me.

Pastor Ghormley told us that his lesson was especially prepared by God in light of what happened in the dining hall. He read to us from Luke 13 Jesus' words, "Make every effort to enter through the narrow door." He went on to say that Jesus wasn't interested in people who had an outward religious appearance without an inward dedication to live by the guidelines God has set down. He said that it's easy to *look* like a Christian—as easy as walking down a wide hallway with no obstacles. But *being* a Christian, finding God's will and doing it, is often as difficult as crawling through a narrow, winding tunnel.

Then he showed us Reverend Stutzman's letter. He said he was afraid those who were involved in the bubble gum rebellion were headed toward the wrong door, the wide door leading away from God.

Suddenly I felt like a living copy of the hymnal I held in my hands—I was very "Christian" looking on the outside, but my insides had been ripped out and stuffed with a lie. I couldn't look up at Pastor Ghormley after that. I almost couldn't breathe!!! I just sat there and stared at the hymnal during the rest of the lesson.

After we were dismissed I found my counselor Maxine and asked if we could talk. In the prayer room I REALLY FELL APART!!! I told her EVERYTHING about the gum, the mattress, the hymnal, and even the part about being like a Bible smuggler. After I had bawled my way through a half a box of Kleenex, Maxine asked me what I thought I should do about my problem. I didn't need to think—I KNEW!!!

She found Reverend Stutzman for me and brought him to the prayer room. It took another half box of Kleenex to tell him the story. In the dining hall before lunch I told the whole camp how sorry I was for causing the trouble by going against the camp rules and missing the "narrow door."

Before I could finish, three guys from cabin 14 stood up at their table and apologized for sending the "letter" to Reverend Stutzman. Then the parade began. Kids standing up all over the dining hall confessing to their leaders and apologizing to each other for their disobedient behavior. There wasn't one dry napkin in the entire dining hall!!! REALLY!!!

This afternoon everybody took part in a massive "gum-out"—collecting very chunk of gum and every piece of wrapper we could find in camp. And tonight at Victory Circle it all went in the fire—wrappers, used gum, and unopened gum. I also tossed the hymnal in the fire. The leather cover is back on my Bible.

Pastor Ghormley talked about the importance of following Jesus through the narrow door when we got back home. Lots of kids got saved tonight, including Darin Keller. If you're wondering what happened to our profits, they are on their way to build a seminary in New Deli (or is it New Delly???). I'm also buying a new hymnal for the chapel and a new pair of jeans for Briget Belcher. I'll pay you what I owe you when I get my allowance. OKAY???

We had a GREAT party after the service tonight. The "Wonderful Grace of Jesus" has never been sung louder. The watered down cocoa and stale marshmallows have never tasted better. AND GUESS WHAT!!! Darin Keller is now going with Brenda Spielmier!!! Wait till somebody tells him how loudly she snores!!! REALLY!!!

Your friend through the narrow door,
Angie

Thought Questions

1. Why do you think Angela had such a hard time realizing that her actions were wrong?

2. Do you know someone who hurts others without realizing it? Could you be in a situation similar to Angela's?

3. Does Angela's experience help you see why the way to salvation is narrow? (See Luke 13:22-27.)

4. Is there anything in your life that is keeping you from entering through the narrow door?

What Are You Doing
New Year's Eve?

"Take my yoke upon you and learn from me, for I am gentle and humble in heart, and you will find rest for your souls." Matthew 11:29

"The December business meeting of the High School Youth Council of the Farley Heights Community Church is now called to order." The words were dutifully recited by the president of the group, Camille Chavez, who punctuated her statement by thumping on the table with her fist in place of a gavel. Sitting around the table with her were the other officers representing the youth group: Vice-President Trent Boorsma, Secretary Ricki Chu, Treasurer Daphne Krueger, and Publicity Chairman Darold Hughes.

"Order? Order?" Darold quipped, wiggling an imaginary cigar in his fingers like Groucho Marx. "I'll have a double cheeseburger, a chocolate shake, and an hour alone with Daffy Krueger." Darold gave Daphne a surprise poke in the ribs which made her jump and yelp. She took a wild, playful swing at Darold, swishing her arm over his quickly ducking head.

"Don't call me Daffy, you creep!" Daphne barked, unable to keep an amused smile from her face.

"Stuff it, you guys. This is a business meeting," Trent rumbled in what he thought was an authoritative, vice-presidential tone. Actually, he sounded like a short-tempered varsity wrestler, which he was.

"What Daffy and I do at this business meeting," Darold stayed in character with his usually entertaining Groucho-ese, "is no business of yours, you big gorilla." This time Darold's poke launched Daphne off her chair with a shriek.

Trent also rose from his chair, looking like an overgrown bulldog ready to chase a pesky cat from his yard. "Shut up, Hughes, or I'll pin your face to the table." Darold immediately raised his hands in mock surrender. He had little respect for "Bulldog" Boorsma as a leader, but plenty of respect for his rippling biceps.

"Come on you guys," Camille pleaded. "We only have an hour before the youth meeting and Pastor Mike wants us to announce our plans for the New Year's Eve party during the meeting." Darold nodded apologetically as he spread a large sheet of paper on the table in front of him to begin sketching ideas for a poster.

"Ricki, would you read the minutes of our last meeting?" Camille looked toward the quiet, dark-haired girl sitting behind a notebook crammed with paper. Ricki started thumbing through her pages when Darold interrupted again.

"Madam chairman," he tried to sound parliamentary and procedural, "I move—and Daffy seconds, don't you Daffy?—that we dispense with the reading of the minutes due to lack of time." Darold had a point. Ricki was so thorough in her note-taking that her minutes seemed to drag on for hours. Her detailed record of past council meetings read like an epic historical novel.

"All in favor please remain seated," Darold continued hastily. "Ah, I see the motion has passed unanimously. Thank you, Ricki," the council comedian added with a wink, "for your support of my good moves."

Trent shot Darold a token glare, but even the bulldog-at-arms was relieved to avoid Ricki's tedious minutes.

"It's a real thrill for me," Ricki smirked sarcastically as she flopped her notebook closed, "to participate in the efficient machinery of high-level government."

"Well then," Camille attempted to gather her troops, hoping Ricki's feelings would survive the mild stomping, "let's get on with the New Year's Eve party."

"I thought last year's party at Mike and Sherie's house was the best party I've ever attended," Daphne said brightly, echoing her simple, naive positivism.

"You want to know why you had such a good time?" Ricki was uncharacteristically bold, hoping that a little bald-faced truth would repay the council for sidestepping her minutes. She didn't wait for an answer. "Because *somebody* in the youth group kept sneaking champagne into your punch glass all evening."

Daphne's face went blank, indicating that her modestly equipped brain was hard at work. "That means I must have been a little drunk and didn't even know it," Daphne exclaimed finally, fascinated by her logical deduction. Daphne had a flair for stating the obvious as if she alone had discovered it.

The *somebody* Ricki referred to squirmed nervously in his chair and his cheeks flushed pink with alarm at the revelation of what had been an airtight secret. Darold noticed Trent's discomfort and smiled to himself, *It's refreshing to see a bulldog reduced to Jell-O in one sentence.* But Darold

wondered why Ricki would mention the champagne incident. And he recalled that Ricki had left the party early last
year.

Like Daphne and Darold, Camille hadn't known about
the champagne either, and she gasped as if witnessing a
violent crime. "Champagne? At a church party? How
awful! Why would someone do that to Daphne?"

Darold, who was more amused than surprised by the
unveiling, answered, "For some it's 'sweets for the
sweet,' but for Daffy it's 'bubbly for the bubble-brain.'"
This time Daphne connected. She lashed out a whip-like
left arm that smacked Darold on the side of the neck.
Unfortunately for Darold, at the moment of impact he was
precariously balanced on the back legs of his chair and the
blow toppled him backwards—arms wildly pinwheeling to
regain his balance—and he landed with a crash on the
hardwood floor.

It took about five seconds to determine that Darold,
his spindly legs intertwined with the chair's legs in a heap,
was unhurt by the fall. Then all five council members burst
into hysterical laughter, complete with tears and side
aches. Daphne crumpled to the floor beside Darold, Trent
sprawled across the table trying to catch his breath, and
Ricki had to leave for the restroom, which incited another
fit of laughter among them.

As the five took their places again at the table several
minutes later, Darold noticed that Camille had regained a
look of mild disbelief on her face. "Hey, Camille," he said
seriously, "you must think that the champagne incident
was the unpardonable sin."

Camille had enjoyed the comic relief of Darold's fall,
but was still stunned by what she had learned. "I've
always been taught that liquor of any kind was absolutely
wrong for the Christian. That's what I thought this church
believed when I came here two years ago. My conscience

would never let me drink a drop of champagne or any alcoholic beverage, let alone sneak it into the glass of a Christian friend."

Darold suddenly realized how little he knew about the convictions of some of his closest friends. But as usual, he had to find the lighter side of even the most serious subjects: "Don't you worry, my little chickadee," his voice was thick with a W. C. Fields accent. "I'm so straight I don't even drink root beer."

But Camille was looking past W.C. Fields. "Do you drink beer and wine and other stuff, Darold?" Her question was direct and inescapable. But before Darold could answer, Camille broadened her question to the rest of the circle by asking, "What do all of you think about drinking?" The group unconsciously leaned closer to each other around the table as if seeking support for a journey into unexplored and previously forbidden territory.

Daphne spoke first, wanting to explain herself since she had been the unwitting victim at the party almost one year ago. "I don't really drink," she began softly, "but it's not a big religious thing with me. I can't stand the taste of the stuff. If my parents have wine for dinner, I may have a sip or two, but that's all I can stomach. I've had some champagne at weddings before but . . . "

"And on New Year's Eve," Darold joked, only faking a jab to her ribs from a safe distance.

"After a couple of swallows my nose starts to sweat and there's a funny buzz in my ears. Come to think of it, I had a headache all New Year's Day last year from the buzzing in my ears."

"And you should have seen the waterfall pouring off your nose!" Darold was Groucho again.

"As I understand it," Daphne continued, obviously thinking very soberly, "the Bible doesn't say, 'Don't drink wine,' but it does say, 'Don't get drunk on wine.' I feel it would be wrong for me to get so involved with drinking that I could be carried away by it. But I don't think I lose my salvation every time my nose sweats."

Darold glanced around the room before he spoke. Camille was still looking at Daphne. The president's face was painted with bewilderment mixed with wonder. Ricki was staring at her notebook, her chin almost resting on her chest. Trent gazed distantly between the heads of the others as if focusing his attention on an object several thousand miles away. "The man I call my dad is really my step-dad," Darold said with a sigh, wishing he was telling a joke instead of revealing something he rarely discussed. "My real dad is an alcoholic. He left my mom when I was only three. As a result, she is completely against any kind of alcohol in the house because she watched it destroy her first husband. She's so straight she won't even cook with wine vinegar." He couldn't resist twiddling an invisible cigar again.

"I've spent enough time with my real dad to know why Mom feels the way she does," Darold continued. "For all I know, I have the same genetic weakness my father has. And if I got involved and went over the falls like my dad, I don't think my mother could handle it. Through all this stuff I think I have heard God saying to me, 'It may be okay for some Christians, but at least for your mom's sake, it's not okay for you.'" Then Darold slipped into the disguise of Fat Albert: "So I don't do no booze no how no way." Camille saw through the disguise, however, and appreciated Darold's honest disclosure.

Ricki had been sitting bowed and motionless for several minutes. She seemed to Darold to be uncomfortable with the subject matter. He called her name and offered her a huge sum of money for her thoughts. She lifted her head with a slight smile and told her story slowly.

"About four years ago my little brother was riding his

bike on the sidewalk near our house. As I was chasing after him to bring him home for dinner, a drunk driver swerved his car onto the sidewalk and hit Bradley. He lasted four days on a machine before he died. It was during the sermon at the funeral that I accepted the Lord and promised God that I would never drink beer or anything because of what happened to Bradley.

"But last year, about a month before the New Year's Eve party, I broke my word." Ricki's head dropped again. "I went on a weekend trip with the ski team and somebody had a keg in their room. I didn't want to look out of place, so I joined in the so-called fun. Later that night we were taking turns driving a snowmobile around the lodge. I didn't think I was anywhere near being loaded so I took my turn at the controls. But I got going too fast and almost hit a kid about Bradley's age.

"That's it, man. Booze is wrong for me physically, socially, mentally, spiritually, every way. Gradually Jesus has taken that burden off my shoulders. But it still rips me up inside to see other kids losing control with the stuff, because I know what can happen."

"So that's why you left the party early last year—you saw the champagne being poured into Daphne's glass," Darold pressed.

"Yeah, I guess I freaked out a little," Ricki answered. "I tried to persuade the *somebody* to ditch the stuff but he said it was just harmless fun. But I know it isn't harmless. And Bradley's funeral was anything but fun. I told the guilty party I wouldn't rat on him if he didn't do it anymore. But for me the party was over, so I left."

"I guess it's my turn now," the words were from Trent who was emerging from a silent battle with himself over how much he was willing to say. Camille, who was absorbing the council's confessions with deep interest, turned and nodded to Trent, encouraging him to speak.

"The *somebody* Ricki is talking about is me, Camille," Trent admitted painfully. Camille hummed her mild surprise. "I knew the champagne thing was bothering Ricki, but I'm glad it came up so I can say some stuff. First, I want to apologize to Daphne for spiking her punch last year." Daphne smiled and shrugged her shoulders, conveying her forgiveness. "And second I want to apologize to Ricki for offending her while I was having my fun with Daphne." Trent was still staring into deep space and his words were dry and unemotional. Darold's humorous side tempted him to start humming the "Battle Hymn of the Republic" for background music, but his serious side held him in check.

"And the third thing I want to say," Trent exhaled a lung full of air, "is that I need your prayers. I drink beer. I drink a lot of beer, in fact. And I've even played around with some hard stuff that would make your warts fall off." Trent was twiddling his thumbs like an old man as he continued his blank stare. But Darold admired the strength he saw in the bulldog's vulnerability.

"When I was a kid," Trent pressed on, "my dad let me finish off his nearly-empty cans and bottles of beer. He thought I was real cute when just a couple of swallows would make me belch real loud. By the time I got to junior high I really loved the stuff. I'd sneak a can up to my room every afternoon and my dad never knew. He was a heavy drinker. The entire house smelled like a brewery.

"I was confirmed in a church where the minister drank beer and the elders served wine at communion—and nobody was hung up on it, especially my dad. When I got into athletics, my skill at the weekly keggers seemed almost as important to the guys on the team as my skill on the mat.

"Now I'm not a six-pack-a-night person," Trent raised his hands as if to swear his innocence. "And I hardly ever get completely bombed out of my gourd. But I sometimes wonder when the brew is going to push me out of the driver's seat. It's like a lot of things Christians can get involved in. Having a few beers may not send me to hell, but a habit like that can be extra baggage to drag along that I really don't need. And after hearing some of you talk, it's baggage that I don't even want any more."

Camille seemed to survive the round of true confessions well. "I guess I never thought there was any reason to stay away from liquor except, 'God will get you if you touch the stuff.' And it looks like we all have similar burdens but God has worked differently in our lives to help us bring those burdens to him and lay them down."

"And there you have it, ladies and gentlemen," Darold was now Howard Cosell, holding a felt marker near his mouth for a microphone. The group smiled at his timely humor. "We've just experienced 30 minutes of brutal honesty the likes of which this reporter has never seen. But the countdown continues—there are only 30 minutes left for this council to plan a New Year's Eve party which promises to be 100 percent non-alcoholic, for the reasons discussed earlier in our program."

Camille exercised the leadership which had brought her to the office of president by reminding the council, "Trent has asked us to pray for him. I think we should do that before we go any further." Camille called upon Jesus to help Trent lay his burden down and find the peace and rest that he sought from God. Darold prayed for the five of them, asking for God's grace to help them lay aside any unnecessary baggage which interferes with following Christ. Then Trent prayed the same prayer for the entire youth group.

In the next 20 minutes Darold completed a colorful poster with felt markers while the council hastily hammered out the details of the youth group's annual New

Year's Eve party. Everything went smoothly until the topic of entertainment came up.

"Let's rent some video movies and stay up all night watching them!"

"Great idea! Let's show that new one, *Blood and Passion*."

"Are you crazy? That movie is rated 'R.' It's full of sex, violence, and raunchy language! We can't show that at a church activity."

"What's wrong with that? Life is full of sex, violence, and raunchy language!"

The volume of the discussion was still rising when Howard Cosell reappeared, microphone in hand. "Here we are, ladies and gentlemen, at the site of another great fight. This time it's the hard-hitting anti-movie goers against the fancy-dancing movie fans. It will probably take several brutal rounds at the next youth council meeting to declare a winner."

In the middle of Darold's sing-songy monologue, Daphne saw the opportunity of a lifetime and took it. With one quick poke at Darold's right elbow, Howard Cosell's microphone scraped across his face, painting half a mustache of blue ink on his upper lip. The early arrivers to the youth meeting couldn't believe finding their council members writhing on the hardwood floor in fitful, crimson-faced laughter.

Thought Questions

1. "Come to me, all you who are weary and burdened, and I will give you rest" (Matt. 11:28). Rewrite this verse in your own words, putting in a burden such as a broken heart or a bad habit that you or someone close to you has experienced.

2. Make a list of several things God would want a person to do in order to find relief from the burden you chose for question number one.

Hark the Herald Angel Speaks

"What good is it for a man to gain the whole world, yet forfeit his soul?" Mark 8:36

Leaving Boise

Tim Shaw gazed over the steering wheel at the narrow, gray carpet of interstate highway stretched out before him in the early morning sunshine. He could not keep the grin on his face from spreading to a full-fledged, toothy smile. Tim had never felt more grateful to God and more proud of himself in the 18 years of his young life. *What a week!* he exulted to himself.

Seven days earlier Tim received his final acceptance papers from the school of his dreams—Melanchthon College of the Bible in Chicago. The letter from the dean of admissions also assured the incoming freshman that a summer job and campus housing were awaiting his late June arrival. Thursday's mail produced another long-awaited treasure—the title to his prized 1978 Dodge van.

After 24 months of budget-crunching payments, Tim's beloved "Vincent Van Go" now belonged to him. Tim had also converted two years' worth of cash gifts from birthdays and Christmases into mag wheels, plush interior, and quadraphonic sound system for "Vinnie."

Then came Saturday—graduation day from Bonner High, and Sunday—Grad Recognition Day at Tim's home church. But best of all was Sunday night after church when the youth group hosted a special farewell pizza bash in Tim's honor. It was so touching that he almost wished he was waiting until fall to journey from the suburbs of Boise, Idaho, to Chicago, Illinois, to begin his college career. *Speaking of touching,* Tim thought with a flush which reddened his youthful cheeks and revived his smile, *how about that good-bye kiss from Prudy Pittman? That was no "greet-one-another-with-a-holy-kiss" type kiss,* Prudy's gorgeous face seemed to materialize on the windshield before him. *That was a full-blown smacker which communicated, "I get excited when I'm close to a college man." Maybe she's been playing hard-to-get all these years,* Tim fantasized.

Tim snapped back to reality when Prudy's image was overcome by a large, green highway sign which zoomed into view and then swished behind the van: LEAVING BOISE. *The party's over,* Tim thought soberly. Tim wasn't sure if it was a wave of spiritual maturity or an early case of homesickness which caused him to decelerate and guide Vinnie to the shoulder of the freeway.

"I'm really going, Lord," he admitted aloud as he draped his arms over the steering wheel and bowed his head. "I'm leaving Bonner, Idaho, my church, my family and," he tried to swallow what seemed to be a tennis ball in his throat, "Prudy Pittman, in order to train for the ministry."

Tim's mind drifted into a deep groove which his fertile imagination had traced countless times over the past months. He saw himself stocking his dorm room with stereo components and oversized speakers, decorating the walls with posters, and settling into the high-speed social life of an independent college man. Then he watched himself receive his bachelor's degree to the wild cheers of the entire population of Bonner, Idaho, which had journeyed to Chicago for his commencement. The scenario continued with Tim driving into the sunset with his bride Prudy to pastor a large, affluent congregation in his denomination.

"But I don't want to waste this summer, Lord," Tim corralled his stray thoughts and continued his prayer. "Use my summer experiences to prepare me for ministry." He was about to pray for Prudy Pittman when he was startled by the heavy rap of bare knuckles on the passenger side window. Tim jerked his head toward the door to see a young man staring at him through the side window. The stranger's head was wreathed by a halo of curly, blonde hair, parted from ear to ear by a pair of stereo earphones with a tiny, foam rubber speaker perched on each cheek.

Before Tim could respond the stranger swung the door open and stuck his head inside. "You're going to Chicago, right?" he asked with a friendly smile.

"Well, yeah," Tim stammered defensively, "but . . . "

"You don't mind if I ride along with you for awhile, do you?" the stranger was not so much asking as telling. "I've got something I need to talk to you about." The young man pulled a knapsack from his shoulder and tossed it between the bucket seats. Then he hopped into the van, closed the door, and buckled into his seat belts. The earphone wires led to a tiny cassette player stuffed in the front pocket of a faded yellow T-shirt. His Levi's were also faded and stringy-thin at the knees. His Nikes looked like they were in need of recapping.

"Do I know you?" Tim asked cautiously as he eased Vinnie back onto the freeway.

"We've never met, Tim," the stranger replied as he reached into his knapsack. "But I know you. In fact, I have an extensive file on you." The young man pulled a three-ring binder from his knapsack and began thumbing hurriedly through a thick wad of pages.

"Who are *you?*" Tim was only slightly more curious than fearful of the bold hitchhiker.

"My name is Hark," the stranger began cheerily, "as in, 'Hark, the Herald Angels Sing.' I am the angel assigned to begin your summer ministry training."

Tim's spine suddenly iced over with fear. *I am alone in the van with a pill head who has been blasted into another brain zone!* he thought frantically. His instincts told him to remain calm, look straight ahead, and pray like crazy.

"It's usually at this point," the man in the passenger seat continued, "that we say something like, 'Fear not,' because for some reason you loved ones of the Master head for Bonkersville when one of us shows up. You are probably thinking that I'm a pill head from another brain zone." Tim did not see the mischievous twinkle in the angel's eye.

Egads! Tim's mind blurted, *he read my thoughts! He's not an ordinary pill head, he's a psychic pill head!* His hands seemed welded to the wheel and he could not bring himself to look at the stranger.

"Actually my full name is Hark Sixty-one Forty-one," the angel continued, unruffled by Tim's frozen panic. "I'm a second tenor in the herald angels choir, which is over 10,000 strong. We're all named Hark, by the way. It's the number which distinguishes us from each other. But since I'm probably the only herald angel you will meet, you can call me by my first name."

Tim's mind was so log-jammed with questions that his

mouth, gaping from shock, didn't know where to start. The angel took advantage of Tim's speechlessness and babbled on with his introduction. "We herald angels form the sanctuary choir and are the primary musicians at all the important events like Creation and the birth of Christ. We presented a dandy cantata at the crossing of the Red Sea." Hark was enjoying the visit.

"You're a musician too, right Tim?" Hark asked. Tim flicked a sideward glance at his rider. "Yeah, I play guitar," he squeaked a nervous reply. Having finally forced himself to speak, Tim continued with a question. "What else do you know about me?" Hark knew Tim was asking a deeper question: "What else do you know about me that only an angel could know?" Tim was grasping for some solid proof.

"I was hoping you would ask," Hark replied. Then he began reading from the notes in his binder. "You have exactly $345.60 in cash in your wallet, plus a check from your parents made out to the college in the amount of $680. Your mother packed you a lunch of four tuna fish sandwiches, two apples, an orange, and three twin-packs of Twinkies, one of which you ate this morning while loading the van." Tim felt his fear melting to breathless wonder. "Your devotions last night were in the eighth chapter of Matthew and you spent most of your prayer time asking the Lord to keep Prudy Pittman safe until you . . . "

"Okay!" Tim cried with such emotion that his hand jerked the steering wheel, causing the van to swerve slightly. "So you're an angel—which is unbelievable, but you know things about me that only God could know!"

"If it's any consolation to you, Tim," Hark encouraged, "most kids your age don't give in so easily. It's a pleasure to work with someone so impressionable."

After several minutes of silence Tim asked the question at the top of his rapidly increasing list: "What's this summer training you're talking about?"

"As I was approaching your van this morning," the angel replied with a compassionate smile, "you were praying that the Lord would prepare you for ministry this summer." Tim nodded, remembering the sincerity of his prayer. "I have brought some assignments to get you rolling in the right direction. I have only one for you today, but we will talk again." The angel closed his notebook and stuffed it in his knapsack. "If you'll pull over here I must be on my way. I have another appointment."

"But what is my assignment?" Tim pressed as he stopped the van, now wishing that the incredible visit had not ended so abruptly.

"You will meet some people today who have a big need that you can meet," the angel spoke clearly and slowly. "When you find them, do what Jesus would do."

"That's it?" Tim queried.

"That's it!" Hark answered. He stepped from the van, turned, and flashed Tim an encouraging smile. "Keep your eyes open, kid." The angel slammed the door and disappeared over the embankment.

For the rest of the morning Tim drove steadily eastward while his mind played an endless tape: *A man in blue jeans and a T-shirt, who carries my life secrets in a notebook in his knapsack, says he's an angel giving me an assignment.* Each time the tape did another lap Tim's logical processes shouted out, *This does not compute! Angels wear linen robes and strum harps! They're too busy keeping heaven running to worry about a pimply-faced kid from Bonner, Idaho.* But fortunately for the young student, something deeper than his logic kept his perplexing objections at arm's length.

Tim did not know what to expect when he pulled off the freeway at 11:30 to buy gas and eat his lunch. *For all I know, everybody I see has a big need,* he thought as he rolled into the gas station and stopped at the pump.

Then, suddenly, there they were—a family of migrant fruit pickers in a dilapidated old station wagon parked at the outside pump. Tim could see the father emptying his pockets of change to buy a few gallons of gas while his wife and four young, dirt-smudged faces watched from inside the car.

Tim sat in his van reluctantly, wishing he was already pastor of an affluent church. *My staff would take care of these kinds of needs,* he told himself. But the words of his angelic visitor rang in his ears: "Do what Jesus would do."

Tim knew enough about migrants to identify their two basic needs: food and enough gas to get to the next farm. He winced as he thought about digging into his carefully budgeted cash. Then he took a deep breath, grabbed his sack lunch, and got out of the van.

He felt awkward offering his lunch to the family, but the father—somewhat skeptical at first—seemed appreciative. Then Tim told the attendant to fill the old car's tank and he would pay the difference from what the father's coins purchased. The glowing faces of the migrant family warmed Tim as he drove away with Vinnie's tank full, but his stomach empty.

As he cruised the highway that afternoon, Tim began to anticipate another visit with Hark. He scrutinized every hitchhiker and stared into every passing car, looking for the youthful face of the angel he had entertained. He was well into Wyoming by sunset, and savored two Quarter-Pounders before looking for a roadside rest to pull into for the night. He had just snuggled into his sleeping bag in the back of the van when a familiar rap on the window startled him.

Tim's flashlight beam through the rear window illuminated the winsome face of his unlikely-looking angel Hark.

"Ooo, it's chilly in this part of the country," Hark exclaimed as he crawled into the van.

"Angels get cold?" Tim wondered out loud.

"Angels visiting the earth in human form feel whatever humans feel," Hark admitted as he gratefully accepted Tim's ski jacket while the youth turned on the van's dome light. The angel sat cross-legged, leaning on the wall.

Tim's curiosity about his angelic visitor had grown through the day and he wanted to know more about Hark than his next assignment. "What kind of music do angels listen to?" Tim asked boldly, pointing to the player in Hark's pocket.

"You mean the cassette?" his visitor asked. "This is really a practice tape for some music we're working on up there." Hark jerked his thumb toward the sky. "We're rehearsing some great tunes for a big banquet coming up. I'm missing a couple of rehearsals while on this mission, so I need to practice my part in my spare time. The tape helps me stay on key. It would be a shame to have a herald angel who didn't know the songs, right?" Hark was almost giggling at his own question.

"Big banquet?" Tim sat up in his sleeping bag, his eyes wide with interest. "When is this big banquet?"

"Wouldn't we all like to know," Hark chuckled. "All I can say is that we have been working pretty hard on these tunes lately and we're almost ready. We're gonna rattle some of those stained glass windows up there!" Then he changed the subject quickly. "You fulfilled your first assignment admirably today, Tim. I'd better give you your next one before I fall asleep. It's been a long day and I must leave early in the morning." He pulled his notebook from the knapsack, located the proper section, and scanned a page in silence. Then he said, "As you might imagine, your training becomes increasingly difficult. That's how you develop your skills in ministry. Tomorrow night you will meet someone who has an even greater need than you witnessed today."

Tim's mind raced ahead to his itinerary for the coming day: continue driving east across the plains to Grand Island, Nebraska, where he would spend the night with Jim and Polly Berry, former youth pastors who had taken the Grand Island church. Tim could not think of any great need which Jim or Polly faced.

"When you recognize the need," Hark continued, starting to yawn, "do what Jesus would do, no matter how hard it may seem."

Tim cleared a place next to him for Hark to lay down, unzipped his sleeping bag, and pulled it over them like a blanket. Hark slid the tiny speakers of his cassette over his ears and Tim turned out the light. In the dark stillness Tim could hear the faint music playing in Hark's ears and his heart pounded excitedly at the reality of his predicament. Finally he poked the drowsing angel and asked, "How long are you going to be training me?"

"It's a day-to-day operation," Hark answered, sounding a little annoyed at the interruption. "I receive a new assignment each day just like you."

"So far I'm doing nothing more than watching for needy people," Tim continued his probe. "When do I get some *real* ministry experience?"

Tim could hear the angel turn his way and he felt his thoughtful gaze in the night. "What do you think ministry is, Tim?" The words seemed to burn into the boy. "In the words of my Master and yours, losing your life daily to meet the needs of others is what it's all about."

Tim wasn't surprised when he awoke and found Hark gone. As he zoomed eastward across Nebraska, he was amazed at how many needs he noticed in the people he encountered. He picked up a very unangelic looking hitch-hiker and treated him to lunch. In a gas station he helped a small boy who was struggling with the air hose while trying to inflate his bicycle tire. Tim realized that these assignments were not from Hark, but somehow he felt right about completing them.

In Grand Island, Tim was warmly welcomed at the parsonage of Jim Berry and his wife, Polly. "You've got a real treat in store for you tonight," Jim announced after the greetings had been exchanged. "We're having a special service tonight at the church with a traveling evangelist and his family." Tim kept smiling, but he wasn't sure a church service was what he needed after 10 hours on the highway.

The service began with a few songs led by the pastor, who then introduced the Clayburne Family. Reverend Clayburne entered from the side room carrying a ratty looking amplifier in one hand hooked up to an even rattier looking electric guitar strapped over his shoulder. He, his wife, and two pre-teen daughters began to sing a medley of upbeat gospel songs with Reverend Clayburne twanging away on the well-worn guitar.

Toward the end of the first music package, Reverend Clayburne's amp started to crackle. The family concluded their medley even though Reverend Clayburne was noticeably disturbed about his equipment failure.

Tim whispered to Jim that he had his guitar in the van and would be glad to set it up for the evangelist's second package of music. Reverend Clayburne beamed at the suggestion, so Tim slipped out during the offertory to retrieve his guitar.

Tim was surprised to find Hark in the parking lot pulling the guitar from Vinnie's rear doors. "Have you spotted a great need yet tonight?" he quizzed his charge.

"Not yet," Tim replied, "unless lending a guitar for five or six songs meets a great need." Then a dark thought entered Tim's mind and he wrinkled his brow at Hark who was wearing a disgustingly angelic grin.

"Not my guitar!" Tim contested loudly. "I use my guitar in ministry. I lead group singing and I hope to get into a singing group at MCB. Besides," Tim felt himself descending to the foundation of his objection, "that guitar and amp cost me 400 bucks!"

Hark shrugged his shoulders sympathetically. "I'm not the one who wrote the assignment." The angel pointed toward the heavens.

"Well I think you've mixed your assignments," Tim said angrily. "God gave *me* this guitar for *my* ministry." Then he turned and stomped back to the church with the guitar and amp.

The quality of Tim's instrument seemed to inspire the Clayburnes during their second package and their music flowed sweetly through the small congregation. Even Tim felt uplifted by their ministry. He knew that his fragile defense was crumbling. The Clayburnes had a great need for his guitar.

Reverend Clayburne preached a short sermon on the theme of giving everything to Jesus. "None of our possessions is going to survive the rapture," he urged, "so we'd better sign them over to Jesus now and use them for His glory." Tim joined several people at the altar that night reaffirming his desire to serve the Lord at all costs.

After the service Tim lingered near the tract rack in the foyer until most of the parishioners were gone and Reverend Clayburne had returned to the platform to pack up. The evangelist thanked Tim for the use of the guitar and amp.

"The Lord spoke to me through what you said tonight," Tim began confidently. "I'd like you to have my equipment for your ministry, sir." Tim couldn't believe what he was saying, but he knew it was right. Reverend Clayburne explained that his family had been praying about better equipment and he thanked Tim for being the vehicle for the answered prayer.

Tim lay awake past midnight in the dark guest room taking mental inventory of his remaining possessions and "signing them over" to the Lord in prayer. It took him more than an hour to let go of Vinnie. Then the soft tap of fingernails on the window caught his attention and he slid from his bed to open the window.

"Your training is going so well," whispered a shivering Hark, "that I have been reassigned to help a missionary in Nepal."

Tim smiled proudly, then said, "Level with me Hark—there is only one assignment: look for needs and meet them, right?"

"In the words of your Master and mine," Hark replied sheepishly, "deny yourself, take up your cross, and follow me."

Tim handed his ski jacket out the window. "You're going to need this in Nepal," he said. Hark thanked him, then turned to leave.

"I will see you at the banquet, won't I?" the angel asked over his shoulder.

"I wouldn't miss it for the world," Tim whispered as he waved good-bye.

Thought Questions

1. Tim was very surprised when God answered his prayer asking for help in preparing for his summer ministry. Yet God answers all prayers. Sometimes God says, "Yes," sometimes He says, "No," and sometimes He answers, "Later." Do you have any prayers that you think God has not answered? Could it be that you are not willing to accept a "No" or a "Later" response from God?

2. God was able to use Tim to help in several situations. Find at least one situation in which God can use you to demonstrate His love today.

3. What possession would be the most difficult for you to give up to the Lord for His purposes? At this point in your life would you be willing to give this possession to God?

There Ain't No Cars in Heaven

"For where your treasure is, there your heart will be also." Matthew 6:21

As a nice Christian boy in high school, I thought that idol worship was mainly frantic chanting and lewd dancing performed by naked heathen in front of naked statues somewhere in the trackless jungle. Since I neither lived in a jungle nor enjoyed dancing, I felt I had about as much chance of becoming an idol worshiper as Elvis Presley had of becoming an opera star.

Then one day my friend Bernie Schalansky drove up to my house in his new '59 Chevy Impala two-door hardtop. It was the most beautiful hunk of Detroit iron I had ever seen—gleaming metallic turquoise body squatting low and wide at the curb; giant teardrop taillights sheltered beneath sweeping, wing-like fins which seemed to spread across two lanes of highway; blinding white leatherette interior oozing the heady, unspoiled fragrance of the show-room. The low-slung roofline crested just above my navel (I was tall for my age) and the sleek, sensuous lines reflected the kind of devil-may-care personality that weakened my knees, inviting me to bow down before the imposing, shimmering, blue-green image.

As if his Impala's natural beauty were not enough of a temptation to idolatry, Bernie had added just the right extras to make his car devilishly celestial—chrome spinner wheel covers; rumble-throated, glass-pack "twice pipes"; and a powerful hi-fi radio blaring 1959's top 40. Bernie's Impala was the kind of car a kid like me would be tempted to sell his soul for. When I slid into the passenger seat I felt like I was entering a pagan temple. Sitting behind the wheel was like offering myself at the altar. I wondered how Bernie—a fine Christian himself—could own such a secular car and maintain an effective Christian testimony. But I forgot all about the issue when he asked if I'd like to double-date with him to the senior prom.

At the time Bernie bought his Impala, I was still driving my first car—a dumpy-looking 1948 Plymouth four-door sedan. It was a lot closer to being a Christian car than Bernie's was, I reasoned, because it didn't drive me to my knees to worship it. Rather, my car kept me on my knees asking for spare parts and money for repairs. Besides, my clunky Plymouth didn't look anything like a god.

By the time Bernie's Impala was three years old, I had bought and sold five different cars with a combined total of more than half a century of highway life. My philosophy was, "buy 'em low, run 'em ragged, sell 'em for scrap iron." Not one of the five looked, sounded, or drove like an Impala.

But as those months and years of automotive tempta-

tion rolled into miles, I discovered something very interesting about myself, Bernie's neat Impala, and my clunky
fleet of cars: any car can become an idol and any car owner
can become an idol worshiper, depending on your point of
view. Jesus must have been speaking to Bernie and me
about idolizing our respective cars when he said, "Do not
store up for yourselves treasures on earth, where moth
and rust destroy, and where thieves break in and steal."
The Impala was especially susceptible to thieves (Bernie
lost three sets of spinners and two radios in the first year
alone!) and my cars were a regular rust factory.

It was during these years in my life when I began to
understand Car-ism—the sinister religion of car worship.
It occurred to me that other youths like myself could be
easily swept into the automotive abyss through the wily
temptations of Impalas, Mustangs, and a variety of customized rods unless somebody revealed Car-ism for the
deceptive cult that it was. So I boldly put my heart in gear,
let out the clutch of my mind, and exposed the false doc-
trines of the car worshipers' faith as listed in the following
categories:

God—The gods of Car-ism are cars, of course, including coupes, sedans, station wagons, convertibles, old,
new, stock, custom, foreign, domestic, and even some
light trucks and vans. Some of these gods are more important than others. For example, my second car—a 1946
Dodge which was about as sleek and sensuous as a gar-
bage truck—was a very minor deity compared to Bernie's
Impala. The only car I knew to be less godly than my
Dodge was my Dad's '53 Nash, an inverted bathtub on
wheels, which was painted brown and green. As a general
rule, the uglier the car, and the more you felt like cursing it
than praising it, the farther down the godhead ladder it
belonged.

I also learned that the car-gods are forever changing

position on the ladder depending on their popularity among the worshipers. It was easy to worship my '48 Plymouth because it was my first car. But when I saw some nice cars owned by my friends, the Plymouth was devalued before my very eyes. Whenever I added some new fru-fru to my car—a set of Mickey Mouse whitewalls, a brodie knob, a plastic gearshift handle, or a chrome-plated air cleaner cover—it rose on the charts. But soon I would see a neater and cooler car than mine and the old Plymouth tumbled down the ladder again. And when Bernie drove up in his new wheels, the '59 Impala immediately became the supreme potentate of cardom, at least until the '60 Fords came out.

Salvation—In Car-ism, salvation is owning a car no matter what you must sacrifice to get it. Signing the title is like filling in a decision card. The registration slip in the glove compartment becomes your certificate of church membership.

For some car worshipers in our youth group, getting "saved" and worshiping the car-god of their choice was a costly decision. It often meant working two jobs, skipping church activities, and ignoring the Bible's teaching about tithes and offerings. I was lucky because none of my first five cars cost more than $125 so it was pretty easy for me to "get saved." However, I was also unlucky because I lost my salvation several times—those cheap cars kept breaking down. I would wander in a state of lostness until I could find another junker and get on the road again. Even though my friend Bernie paid through the nose for his Impala, he was "eternally secure," at least for several years.

Worship—As in any religion, worship in Car-ism means giving yourself totally and unreservedly to your god. You can always identify true car worshipers by how much time they spend washing, waxing, cruising in, or bragging about their cars. Car idolizers know for sure that any activity involving a car is superior to such humdrum non-essentials as eating, sleeping, or homework. Most zealots can swerve any conversation onto their cars in less than five minutes. And for the devout, the means always justifies any end. It's never, "I want to go to the store so I will drive the car," but rather, "I want to drive the car so I will go to the store" (or the movie, animal shelter, grandmother's house, morgue, or wherever).

Servants of the car-gods can also be distinguished by the offerings they bring to their images. There is no end to the goodies and gadgets that car owners can buy which will make their gods faster, shinier, higher, lower, comfier, noisier, quieter, or more or less fuel efficient. Some cars have every new chrome this and special electronic that imaginable, and yet their doting subjects worshipfully lavish gifts upon them strictly out of devotion. For example, a car may have a perfectly good set of tires, but the loving owner pays hundreds of dollars for a set that is wider or has the right brand name lettered on the side. Another car may be equipped with an adequate engine, but the devoted worshiper will spend unselfishly in order to provide his god with more cubic inches, horsepower, mph's, or rpm's.

I was a tight-fisted giver to the five minor gods I served while Bernie adored his Impala with an endless stream of offerings. But my heart was in the right place. If I'd had more to spend on my cars I would have spent more. But I did humbly offer to them rubber floor mats (even though the floors were already rubberized), chrome gas caps, a bell mounted under the front floorboard which I could ring by stomping a plunger with my left heel (the electric ooga-ooga horns drained the battery and were too expensive), and various other doodads which showed my peers that I was a sincere, albeit poor, car worshiper.

Sin—For the car freak, sin is thinking that a vehicle is

nothing more than a mode of traveling from one point to another. In reality, transportation is merely incidental to a car's true purpose: establishing an identity. Car worshipers realize that their wheels are as much a part of their identity as their birth certificates or Social Security cards. My friend Bernie Schalansky was no Rock Hudson in looks or personality. But Bernie *plus* his Impala added up to at least a Tab Hunter in the eyes of our crowd. And I wasn't exactly a dating machine in those days. But without my modestly customized clunkers I probably wouldn't have been close enough to a girl to smell her perfume until I was out of college. In Car-ism, your car is as important as your face, arms, or legs. You're crippled without it.

Grace—In the world of cars you pretty much get what you deserve. If you work hard and save your money, you can buy a nice Impala like Bernie did. If you are scraping along on meager earnings and dribbling much of that away on French fries and cherry Cokes, you'll end up driving something like my third car—a '49 Mercury four-door for which I paid $85. It was lowered to the ground and looked like a cross between a World War II tank and a gangland limousine. The driver's door was jammed shut and the right front wheel was bent at such an angle that it chewed up a cheap retread tire every month. The Merc burned almost as much oil as it did gas, and billowed enough smoke to single-handedly increase the ozone count in our community.

Bernie got what he deserved and I got what I deserved.

But sometimes you stumble into something better than you deserve, like when our youth sponsor at church let me borrow his classic midnight black '57 Chevy Bel Air hardtop to take Olivia Brewster to the big game. There I was slowly cruising the black Chev through Bimbo's Drive-In after the game, with Olivia perched by my side.

Ordinarily I would have been alone in the Merc laying a smoke screen which probably would have resulted in my ejection from the drive-in. That's grace!

I was the recipient of grace again shortly after the Merc died of carburetor cancer and was sold for junk. (I had brought so much business to the wrecking yard that the owner treated me like a son!) All my friends were buying and customizing '50 Chevies, including Dave McMurphy—the Adonis of the youth group—who dropped a hefty GMC truck engine into his little Chevy.

But at this point in my life I was rebelling against the car-gods, so I settled for a less auspicious '50 Plymouth sedan which I purchased for $100. It was a clean, low-mileage, sweet-running "Grandpa and Grandma" car. Yielding to one of the fads of the day, I took the car to a local sign painter and had the words "Little Fury" inscribed on both rear fenders.

To my surprise, my well-cared-for Plymouth had a spunky engine that could keep up with most of the Chevies in our youth group. Realizing that the grace of the Plymouth-god was upon me, and emboldened by the soft warmth of Ellen Bushbaum by my side, I challenged Dave McMurphy to a drag race down Anson Avenue after church one Sunday night. I had a great start, a fantastic speed-shift into second, and was leading by half a car length when I jammed into third gear. Suddenly, Dave and his Jimmy-powered Chevy dropped back. "He's giving up!" I exulted proudly to Ellen. "I've whipped the fastest Chevy in the youth group! Amazing grace!"

But Ellen hadn't heard me. Her bulging eyes were welded to a stop sign which we roared through at almost 70 miles per hour. My balloon of elation exploded as I soberly realized that I could have killed myself, Ellen, and anyone who might have chanced to cross Anson Avenue as I approached, not to mention reducing "Little Fury" to a little wad of scrap metal. My admiration for my car was suddenly swallowed up in a sheepish appreciation for God and His infinitely superior grace.

As I departed from my teen years I squirmed out of the grip of the car worshiper mentality which had terrorized me as an adolescent. My escape was aided by my continuing poverty—I could never afford a major league, status-enriching car-god. But more important, I began to understand what Jesus meant by treasures which were vulnerable to moths, rust, and thieves. By this time even Bernie's heavenly Impala was showing signs of wear and tear.

Once free of the domination of the car-gods, I overreacted. Instead of being my idols, suddenly cars became my enemies—the residue of the original sin on a par with weeds, thorns, smog, ingrown toenails, hemorrhoids, and baldness. After all, what possible spiritual value can be found in a device which brings you flat tires, dead batteries, burned out clutches, leaky radiators, or broken timing chains? *There ain't no cars in heaven,* I reasoned to myself. *If God had wanted us to drive He would have given us wheels instead of feet.*

But the pendulum soon swung back to center and I began to accept cars for what they are—instruments which, if used correctly, can assist us in securing treasures which are impervious to rust, moths, or thieves. I bought a very ungodly-looking economy car which impressed few of my peers but allowed me to save enough money to enter Christian college in preparation for pastoral ministry.

Since then I have owned eight different cars—most of them modest and functional, and none of them as classy as I remember Bernie's Impala to be more than 25 years ago. I have a wife who loves me for who I am rather than for what I drive, and we have two teenage children who are successfully overpowering the car-gods which tempt them. I think we understand that it's okay to own any car—from a clunker to a Cadillac—as long as the car doesn't own us.

I still have a dream car, however—a 1972 Buick Riviera, with its distinctive, sloping, V-shaped rear deck. I wouldn't mind owning one someday, but it's so hard to find one that isn't starting to rust.

Thought Questions

1. Jesus advised us to lay up treasures in heaven rather than treasures on earth (see Matt. 6:19). Identify any earthly "treasures" that make it hard for you to obey Christ's advice.

2. List the sort of things you could do or be that would produce "heavenly treasures."

The Treaders of Terrabon

"But seek first his kingdom and his righteousness, and all these things will be given to you as well.". Matthew 6:33

In the not-so-distant land of Terrabon there lived a large and happy clan of nomads called the Treaders. Although the good Lordmaster of Terrabon had deeded to the Treaders more square miles of territory than they could possibly visit in a lifetime, the wandering clan called no place their home, preferring the adventure and discovery of life on the trail. Their destination was the exquisite castle of the Lordmaster himself which was perched somewhere above the clouds atop Terrabon's highest peak.

The clan's legendary vanguard was the Fronter, who lovingly and wisely directed the Treaders on their daily journeys. Without the Fronter's leadership and provision, the Treaders would have long since forsaken the rigors of the trail and settled for the uneventful existence of the lazy Stayheres, who had established the villages in Terrabon. The Stayheres could not understand why the Treaders chose to ignore the comforts of the village to ascend a perilous peak looking for a castle which could not be seen from the valley floor. The Treaders, however, inspired by the Fronter, refused to compromise their glorious quest— the magnificent domain of the Lordmaster.

The Treaders were such a large clan that they never congregated in one place, but rather tramped during the day and camped at night in a line which stretched out for miles on the trail. The Fronter always walked a few hundred feet ahead of the clan preparing the trail and locating the provisions which the Lordmaster had stored along the trail for those who braved the mountainside to seek him.

It was not difficult for the Treaders to keep a brisk pace on the trail because they carried only the garments which they wore. If his garment wore thin, a Treader needed only to pass a request up the line and the Fronter, who knew where the Lordmaster had stashed such supplies along the trail, would secure the needed garment and pass it down the line within a day or two. The Treaders slept warmly each night on a soft bed of rillwood boughs wrapped in blankets of giant, fuzzy oomdraw leaves.

Each morning the Treaders awoke to find a bountiful supply of food for the day provided by the Fronter at the trail head. The nourishing fruits, vegetables, and nuts were quickly passed down the line until every clan member had filled the pouch belted to his waist with enough provisions for three meal stops each day.

After each day's firstmeal, the Treaders would scour the hillsides near their trailsite collecting rare and beautiful abix stones—small, brilliantly colored gems which could be found in the clover among the acres of blooming fipwadders and ethilias. The prized abix were eagerly sought by the Treaders as gifts to be presented to the Lordmaster upon their arrival at his castle. An average Treader was lucky to find one or two abix a month which they carefully secured in their pouches in anticipation of journey's end. With the security of the Fronter's daily provision in their hearts and a sprinkling of newly found abix in their pouches, the Treaders began each day's trek with joy and enthusiasm. Flocks of blue-crested stoomers chirped and flitted through the trees in celebration of each morning's departure.

Somewhere in the middle of the long line of marchers were three Treaders named Skad, Grubble, and Bim. One day as the clan rested for midmeal, the three fellow-travelers engaged in simple conversation on the most popular themes among Treaders—the anticipation of reaching the Lordmaster's castle and the gratitude they felt for the Fronter's leadership and provision.

"This is an exceptionally fine midmeal the Fronter has provided today," said Bim as he split open a small miltermelon and gouged out the seeds with his bare hands.

"He knows what we like to eat," Grubble added, rotating a ripe drellafruit in his hand, anticipating his first bite. "I don't know what we'd do without him as our vanguard."

Skad, who was the brightest of the three, sat on the ground in quiet determination, cracking open several hubbapods between two stones. With his concentration loosely fixed on such a mundane task, Skad was suddenly surprised by a dark thought which snared his mind as if he had walked into the sticky web of one of the forest's knabbit creepers. Before he quite understood the thought which had arrested him, he voiced it to his partners: "What if the Fronter was unable to supply our food?"

Skad's question startled his fellow Treaders. Bim

dropped half his melon and Grubble stopped chewing, his cheeks stuffed with the first big bite of drellafruit.

"What a terribly horrible thought," Bim gasped disbelievingly.

"Terribly horrible," Grubble echoed. Indeed, such an audacious idea had never been entertained or voiced by a Treader before.

"We have always assumed that our provisions will be passed down the line every day without fail," Skad restated his thought as it grew cancerously in his mind. "But what if a day dawns and nothing comes down the line? We are totally dependent upon the Fronter for our sustenance. What if he is not as dependable as we think?"

The same web which had captured Skad's imagination quickly wrapped itself around Bim and Grubble and the frightful possibilities began to multiply.

"The Fronter could miss the Lordmaster's stash and we would be without food for an entire day," Grubble advanced, a cloud of worry spreading over him.

"Or he might take the wrong fork in the trail and we would be without food for an entire week!" Bim moaned, trembling.

"But such a thing has never happened!" Grubble tried to sound confident.

"But who says it never will?" Bim countered fretfully. The three friends sat in silence as their fears threatened to carry them away.

Skad bravely assumed command of the situation and his two friends. "We must take care of ourselves," he said bravely. "We must insure our own provisions in case of a failure at the front."

"But how do we do that?" Grubble whimpered, clutching his once-bitten drellafruit as if it was his lastmeal. "We have always depended on the Fronter."

"We will still accept what comes down the line," Skad

assured, "but we will also begin to acquire a reserve supply of provisions in case of emergency."

"Where will we find provisions?" Bim wore a look of mild despair.

"In the Stayhere villages along the trail," Skad announced. "We'll trade abix stones for fruit and pods."

"But we're collecting abix for the Lordmaster," Bim breathed reverently.

"Listen to me," Skad whispered gruffly, trying to emphasize his point without alarming others along the trail. "If we don't trade for provisions we may never live to see the Lordmaster."

Bim and Grubble nodded submissively. Then the three of them savored the last bites of their midmeal and made sure enough remained in their pouches for dinner.

Late that afternoon the Treaders' trail wound through a small Stayhere village. Skad, Grubble, and Bim stepped out of line—though urged not to do so by their fellowtravelers—and approached a marketplace. For one brilliant abix they were able to fill their pouches with fruit and pods common to the Treaders' diet. But the merchants displayed tempting delicacies which were very seldom found on the trail—yumcane cakes, bontop shoots, and spiced blinta meat. For another abix they bought several delicious cakes, a few hunks of spiced blinta, and a new pouch to carry them in. They rejoined the clan, having lost several places in line, with their bulging pouches bobbing at their belts.

The next morning the Fronter's provisions arrived as usual. But after eating the firstmeal the three wary Treaders were unable to find room in their pouches to carry their other two meals. They stuffed their stomachs with more than they were hungry for and stowed additional foodstuffs inside their garments. With impending famine lurking in their minds, the trio was not about to abandon even the tiniest morsel of food.

At midmeal a garment came down the line which Grubble had requested two days previously. All three friends stiffened with the same thought but it was Grubble who voiced it: "There may come a day when the Fronter is unable to provide the garments we need."

"Freezing from lack of cover is as bad as starving from lack of food," Bim deduced carefully. Skad agreed with them and they determined to trade abix for additional garments in the next village.

It was two more days before they reached the next Stayhere community. Reminding themselves that starvation may be waiting for them just up the trail, Skad, Grubble, and Bim eagerly traded an abix for a stalk of granchweed, a variety of nuts and pods, and a leg of roast burrybeast. They also purchased three large baskets with handles in order to carry their growing larder.

They dragged their baskets to the local weaver who displayed a variety of brightly colored garments. Skad and his friends marveled at the fabrics and designs which made their own garments seem drab in comparison. They dug deeply into their pouches and traded several abix for two garments each, which they tied into bundles and carried on their shoulders as they hurried to get back into line.

During lastmeal the three shoppers were the talk of the line as they stepped from the bushes elegantly robed in Stayhere finery, and then dined on the exotic foods from their pouches and baskets. After the meal they were surrounded by a score of their clansmen who pelted them with criticism.

"Why do you spend the Lordmaster's abix on unnecessary food and garments?"

"The Fronter knows what we need and will supply it as he has always done."

"You're carrying too much baggage and you're getting

fat! You'll not be able to keep up the pace on the trail!"

"It is not right for Treaders to copy the ways of the Stayheres!"

But Skad, Grubble, and Bim reclined beside their campfire, patting their rounded bellies and commending themselves on their wisdom and foresight. "The Fronter delivered today," they agreed, "but he may not deliver tomorrow. And we are the only Treaders in the clan who are ready."

As the days passed, the three skeptical travelers continued to spend their abix freely at every village where Stayhere merchants hawked succulent taste treats and fine garments. Their pouches and baskets swelled to the breaking point and their garment bundles towered over their heads. They discarded their simple Treader wraps and arrayed themselves in new Stayhere garments every day. They gave up trying to salvage the Fronter's daily food supply, preferring to dine on the delectable meats and sweets which made all the Fronter's food seem as tasteless as frackroot gruel.

It took the three friends so long to dress and load up their treasures each morning that they had no time to join in the daily search for abix among the fipwadders and ethilias. As the Lordmaster's treasure increased in the pouches of other Treaders it diminished in the pouches of Skad, Grubble, and Bim. Try as they might to keep their place in line, the three burdened Treaders staggered heavily along the trail while their unencumbered fellow-travelers strode by them with ease.

One late afternoon the trail around Skad, Grubble, and Bim became quiet except for the panting and wheezing which accompanied each of their halting steps. The last of the Treader clan had passed them by. They were alone on the trail, dropping farther behind the line with each unsteady step.

Panicked at being left behind, they tried to quicken their pace, only to collapse more often in need of rest. They ate and slept that night on the trail, and rose early to make up for lost time. But they reached a fork in the trail and the Fronter's markings had been erased by hundreds of tramping feet. They took the path which seemed to wind toward the mountain, but after several miles the trail dipped and descended into the valley. Another fork appeared, and another, and another. With each confused choice the trio stumbled farther into the valley. The trail became narrower and darker as the overhanging branches blotted out the beautiful mountain and then the sunlight itself. Suddenly the trail ended in a dark, dismal grove of muggerwood trees. The three misled travelers fell to their knees in despair, spilling their pouches and baskets carelessly and dumping the heavy bundles of garments from their shoulders.

"What do we do now, Skad?" Grubble and Bim whined together. "We are hopelessly lost. We will never find the clan. We will never see the castle or present our last few stones to the Lordmaster of Terrabon."

Skad yearned to offer his friends some hope, but he had none left to give. "We have nowhere to go," he sighed. "We will have to stay here."

"Stay here?" Grubble and Bim croaked loudly. "But we are not Stayheres—we are Treaders!" The ugly truth of their predicament fell heavily upon them and they moaned fitfully.

"We are Treaders who have foolishly thought like Stayheres," Skad confessed finally. "We were born to sweep along the trail, collect the beautiful abix, and seek the Lordmaster. Instead we shall die in this miserable valley leaving only a worthless collection of Stayhere treasures as a tombstone." The suffocating darkness closed around the trio and they buried themselves remorsefully in a huge pile of garments, miltermelons, yumcane cakes, and granchweed stalks.

Suddenly they heard a noise on the trail behind them. *A wild beast! A robber!* they each feared independently. Burrowing more deeply into the pile of Stayhere stuff, Skad, Grubble, and Bim each kept one eye uncovered, staring into the darkness of the trail. Through the muggerwoods they saw a flicker of torchlight and soon the figure of a lean and trim traveler came into view. Then the visitor was standing over the heap, torchlight illuminating his face. It was the Fronter.

"Don't be concerned about surviving on the trail," the Fronter began after gently pulling the three shame-faced Treaders from their grave of Stayhere goods. "Isn't the purpose of our journey more important than the provisions needed to complete it? Think about the blue crested stoomers and the warbling bicknuggles which soar through the heavens. They have no pouches around their waists, yet the Lordmaster adequately feeds them. And the Lordmaster esteems even the weakest Treader above the simple stoomer." Skad, Grubble, and Bim felt so ashamed for ignoring the Fronter's provision. But somehow they knew he understood and his words soothed them and lifted their spirits.

"And what about the blooming fipwadders and delicate ethilias?" the Fronter continued, the torchlight glistening in his clear, dark eyes. "They don't carry bundles of garments on their backs, yet there isn't a weaver alive who could make a garment as beautiful as a fipwadder's cloak. And the Lordmaster esteems even the smallest Treader above the lowly fipwadder."

The Fronter handed Skad his torch and began pushing the Stayhere merchandise into a tall pile as he concluded his speech. "A Treader is not to concern himself unduly with food and garments as the short-sighted Stayheres do.

Rather, set your attention on the trail, the abix which surround it, and the Lordmaster's welcome at its end. I will make sure you have what you need to complete the journey."

The Fronter finished preparing the pile of garments and foods, then looked at the torch in Skad's hand. The Treader knew what to do.

It took nearly an hour for the pile to burn to the ground. With each leaping flame Skad, Grubble, and Bim felt the weight of their former worries lift from their minds. They were free to be Treaders again and trust the Fronter for everything.

Each Treader made a torch for himself from a muggerwood branch swathed with saffy moss. Then they began climbing the trail to rejoin the clan, following the Fronter and watching for abix along the path.

Thought Questions

1. List the things modern Stayheres might put in their pile.

2. Why do you think we are asked not to be concerned with material things?

3. Do you honestly think you could be content with food and covering? Why or why not?

Bombs Over Malibu

"'Love the Lord your God with all your heart and with all your soul and with all your mind and with all your strength . . . . Love your neighbor as yourself.' There is no commandment greater than these." Mark 12:30,31

Chad Nichols shoved a wrinkled $10 bill across the counter to the impish freshman girl who had just plopped six hot dogs and three Cokes in front of him. "Let's see, six at 75 cents and three at 50 cents," she began drumming her forehead with her fingers as if calculating the sum on her frontal lobe. Above the snack bar the bleachers thundered with the cheers and stomps of the North Valley student body urging their Grizzlies toward another touchdown.

"C'mon, shrimp!" Chad demanded, pounding on the bill. "You're gonna take all night! It's six bucks for everything!" The lanky blond senior stuffed one of the hot dogs into his mouth and chomped it in half. The freshman girl, frazzled and flushed, continued to calculate. "Six bucks! Six bucks!" Chad insisted impatiently, his cheeks swollen with half a hot dog and his chin smeared with mustard. The girl squeaked a near-tears sigh, grabbed the bill, threw four singles on the counter, and turned to escape.

"Hey, shrimp! How am I supposed to carry this stuff?" Chad interrupted her retreat loudly. The girl squealed angrily and threw an empty bun carton toward Chad before disappearing behind the Coke machine. "Service with a smile," Chad joked toward the students in line, his cheeks bulging with the rest of his first hot dog.

A huge cheer exploded from the bleachers as Chad, balancing hot dogs and Cokes, threaded his way up the stairs. He edged into his crowded row and squeezed into a seat between his two friends. "What happened, Ruderman?" he quizzed.

"Buford, of course," Ruderman answered, his attention drawn to the two hot dogs which Chad thrust toward him. "He blasted up the middle for about 20 yards."

"What a rhino!" Reggie McGill added. "He must be over a hundred yards already." McGill's last few words were drowned by another cheer as Buford Steele, the powerful fullback, bounced off a tackler at the line of scrimmage, spun to his right, and rumbled over a fallen blocker for seven more yards.

By the start of the fourth quarter, Buford Steele and the Grizzlies had the game well in hand. "I wonder if Bufe can really make it at UCLA," McGill mused aloud as he folded his program into his version of the Concorde.

"They're already recruiting him," Chad answered authoritatively. "And he'll pick UCLA alright. He wants to play in the same backfield with T.J." Ruderman and McGill grunted their agreement.

Chad flashed back to his freshman year at North Valley—joining the crowds jamming the stadium on Friday nights to watch Buford's leaner and faster brother T.J. streak to high school all-American honors before starring as a freshman at UCLA. "I'll never forget the day," Chad voiced his vivid memory, "when T.J. got us into the Southern Cal game."

"The Bruins have a bye tomorrow," Ruderman interrupted the nostalgia, "so T.J. will be home this weekend. We ought to hit him up for tickets to the Oregon game."

"So if he's in town this weekend," McGill began as he launched his paper plane toward the litter-strewn track, "why isn't he here watching his little brother stomp all over Edison?"

"T.J.'s girlfriend has a brother who plays for Santa Monica City College," Chad informed. "If he's smart he went to the Santa Monica game with his woman."

When the coach started pulling the first stringers out of the game, Chad, McGill, and Ruderman climbed into Ruderman's '68 VW bug which headed for the Pizza Den as if on auto-pilot. "This night is begging for some action," McGill said as he slid open the sun roof and welcomed the Indian summer breeze. "We haven't made a bombing run since . . . when? Last May? Let's get some balloons and boogie for Malibu." McGill's friends howled with anticipation.

It took Chad's last four dollars to buy out 7-11's supply of balloons and it took the three boys nearly an hour to fill them with water and load them carefully—in two large buckets—into the back seat of the bug. By 11 P.M. they were speeding north on the freeway toward Malibu Canyon Road and a 20-minute drive to the coast. There the Malibu cliffs overlooked narrow, fluorescent beaches dotted with the campsites of unsuspecting targets.

"Buford says T.J. has changed a lot since he started at UCLA," Chad yelled from the back seat as the roaring engine and swirling wind baffled conversation.

"You'd change too," McGill called back from the front, "if you had pro scouts charting how you brush your teeth and sorority maidens clawing after your body." McGill and Ruderman whooped with envy.

"No, I mean T.J.'s more serious about life and stuff," Chad himself felt uncharacteristically serious for a moment. "Buford says T.J. doesn't party like he used to; says he's involved in one of the Christian campus groups."

"Hallelujah!" Ruderman shouted, waving one hand out of the open sun roof. "What a waste of human life!" McGill added a sanctimonious sounding, "Amen!"

Chad thought about issuing one more invitation to a serious conversation, but quickly changed his mind as his two friends began discussing the merits of the UCLA cheerleading squad. Instead, he leaned back between the two buckets and retreated into a cavern of deep thought.

T.J. Steele's new image had made more of an impact on Chad Nichols than he was ready to admit. The UCLA star tailback had once been the king of the North Valley party jocks whose motto was, "beer, bennies, and babes." But as a freshman at UCLA, T.J. roomed with a cornerback who was even deeper into the Bible than T.J. was into the three *B*'s. By the end of the football season, Buford had reported to Chad, T.J. was toting a Bible, spouting verses, and his medicine chest contained nothing stronger than generic aspirin.

"T.J. says the Bible can be summarized in five words," Buford said to Chad one spring day as they walked from chemistry to the cafeteria. "Love God and love people— that's it! That's the whole Bible!" *T.J.'s religion is obviously leaking into his little brother,* Chad thought that day, feeling uncomfortable. But what really bothered Chad was when, later that week, Buford declined his invitation to a bombing run on Malibu Beach by saying, "It wouldn't be the loving thing to do."

Water bombing Malibu Beach is harmless, clean fun, Chad insisted to himself as Ruderman navigated the off-ramp at Malibu Canyon Road and began to accelerate the VW up the gradual, winding incline into the canyon. For a few more minutes, at least, Chad believed himself.

The air flowing into the car was rich with the fragrance of sagebrush and the moon spotlighted the northern wall of the canyon from a cloudless sky. The cooling temperature charged the three friends with excitement and Chad startled himself with a brilliant idea. "Hey," he chirped mischieviously, "watch this!" Chad pulled himself into a squatting position on the rear seat and grabbed a water balloon. The headlights of an approaching car emerged from behind the canyon wall and Chad flipped the bulging balloon out of the sun roof and into the opposite lane. The station wagon sped under the balloon's arc and Chad watched his bomb splatter on the moonlit pavement.

"Ooo-eee!" shrieked McGill. "Give me a couple of those things!" Chad placed two water balloons into McGill's eager hands and grabbed another for himself.

"All right! A mobile bombing mission!" Ruderman sang excitedly, downshifting to third as the incline increased and the turns became tighter. The next pair of headlights appeared around the curve. Again Chad's launch was late, while McGill's first hook shot out the side window nearly fell through the open sun roof, splashing just behind Chad's periscoping head. The next two cars barely escaped a volley of missiles from the bombers, but they both found the mark on a third car.

"I think I got the driver's door," McGill exclaimed.

"I got him too," Chad triumphed, "right in the middle of the grille."

The VW roared past the midway point between the valley and the coast and began a gradual decline, picking up speed. Challenged by his success, Chad rose from his crouch, braced his right knee on McGill's seat back and lifted himself out of the sun roof almost to his waist. The brisk headwind pushed tears to the corners of his squinted eyes and unfurled his blond hair behind him as if it were starched.

"Oncoming target!" Ruderman barked as a pair of headlights snaked around the bend a quarter mile ahead of them.

"Ammo! Ammo!" Chad chanted, reaching down toward McGill.

Chad received two water balloons from McGill just in time to shovel them both on a low arc into the path of the passing car, an older model white Porsche coupe. Both balloons exploded on the windshield. "Direct hit!" Chad exulted, both arms raised in victory.

"Oh no!" Ruderman screamed, his eyes glued to the rear view mirror. "I think he's stopping!" Chad jerked his head around to see two brilliant brake lights illuminating a cloud of dust alongside the road several hundred feet behind them. The taillights slid out of view and were replaced by two shafts of searching white light as the Porsche fishtailed violently onto the westbound lane in the distance.

"He's coming after us!" Ruderman cried. "What are we gonna do?" The pursuing Porsche dropped out of sight momentarily as the roadway wound around an interposing canyon wall.

"Step on it! Move this thing!" Chad commanded as he dropped to the back seat and slammed the sun roof closed. Panic and fear, mixed with rabid excitement, jolted the three boys like a drug and their mouths babbled freely.

"Stand on it, Ruderman! Move it! Move it!"

"It's only eight miles to the coast! We can lose him in Malibu!"

"If that Porsche is hot it can catch us in one mile!"

"What if he has a gun! What if he's a cop!"

"Go, Ruderman! Go!"

As Ruderman squealed the VW into each bend in the road Chad and McGill leaned hard to the inside of each turn. Every few seconds one of them would strain a look out the rear window to see the high beams of the Porsche peek-a-booing menacingly from behind the rocky canyon walls.

"I think he's gaining on us a little!" Ruderman yelled as the speedometer climbed to 70. He felt as though his foot was going to push the accelerator through the floor.

"It's only about two miles to the coast highway," McGill estimated. "But where do we go then?"

"Let's head north toward the cliffs," Chad offered. "He will probably turn south hoping to catch us on the road into Malibu. If we reach the north fork before he spots us we should be home free." McGill and Ruderman, groaning at the lack of alternatives, resigned themselves to Chad's plan.

The Porsche had been out of sight behind them for almost a minute when Ruderman steered the roaring VW northbound onto the coast highway. The lights of Malibu sparkled behind them. Three pair of eager eyes watched the dark ribbon of highway escaping beyond the back window as the car raced northward.

After almost two miles on the coast highway McGill broke the silence: "I think you were right, Chad. We've lost him! We've won the German Gran Prix!" The three boys exulted loudly over their victory. Shortly, Ruderman guided the VW into a rest area, parked between two 18-wheelers, and shut off the lights.

"I don't know what that dude could have done if he *had* caught us," Ruderman speculated, suppressing his dwindling fear with an injection of synthetic courage. "There couldn't have been more than two of *them* in that coupe and there are three of *us*."

"Yeah," McGill boasted. "Let's go back and find that guy and get him again."

But Chad suddenly began to feel uncomfortable—like he had when Buford Steele explained T.J.'s five-word summary of the Bible. He found himself thinking seriously for the second time that night—this time about himself and what he had just done.

The VW and the Porsche could have easily plunged into the canyon on one of those daredevil curves. Or we could have been snagged by the cops and hauled off to jail for reckless driving, he realized soberly. *And somewhere back in the valley,* Chad's thoughts continued to snowball, *there's a tiny freshman girl crying to her mother about the creep who humiliated her at the snack bar.* Chad doubted that T.J. Steele would have done what he did tonight, and somehow that thought made him wish he could start the night over again.

Chad convinced his friends that they should dispose of the incriminating evidence. They dumped the rest of the water balloons in the sagebrush behind the rest area. Then Chad curled up in the back seat and rode home in fitful silence.

Chad suspected that the mid-morning phone call was for him even before his mother brought the phone into his room. He pulled his head out from under his pillow and picked up the receiver. "Hello."

"Chad, this is Buford," echoed the husky voice on the phone.

"Yeah, hi Bufe," Chad mustered a hopeful greeting.

Buford's question was immediate and pointed: "Did you go bombing last night?" Chad stiffened, wishing that the events and feelings of the previous night would have evaporated while he slept. He swung his legs out from under the covers and sat tentatively on the bedside.

"Yeah, I did," he admitted remorsefully, ready to confess his dissatisfaction with himself over the issue. "But I . . ."

"Chad?" a deeper voice came on the line. "This is T.J." The voice on the other end of the phone was steady and serious. "Chad, my girlfriend and I drove home from Santa Monica last night over Malibu Canyon Road." Chad instantly knew what was coming and his heart dropped to his ankles. "Somebody in the other lane threw some water balloons at our car," T.J. continued. "The impact cracked the windshield and I nearly drove off the road." Chad gasped and the serious voice paused as if inviting a confession. *Why did it have to be T.J.?* Chad pleaded silently. "Do you know anything about it?" T.J. concluded.

Chad felt a powerful fist of guilt punch him in the stomach. He wished he was in Alaska. He wished he were dead. Then he wished he could talk to T.J. about what happened to his idol when he joined the Christian group at UCLA.

"White Porsche?" Chad breathed slowly after a convicting silence.

"Yeah, it belongs to my girlfriend Jeri. She's pretty upset."

"Gee, I'm sorry T.J.," Chad's apology was painfully genuine and his voice began to quaver with emotion. "I didn't realize water balloons could crack a windshield. I'll pay for the damage—I'm really sorry."

"When those balloons hit, man, I really went crazy," T.J. spoke again. "I didn't know who was in the VW, but I drove after you like a wild man. Jeri finally talked me down before we reached the coast highway. When we got to the folks' house and told the family about it, Buford said he had an idea who might have done it. He said he used to go bombing with you."

"I caused you a lot of trouble, T.J.," Chad searched for

another way to vent his penitence.

"Hey, it's over, man," T.J. cut him off. "I accept your apology and I forgive you. When we get the bill for the windshield, I'll bring it over."

Chad tried to verbalize his regret several more times. But T.J. rebuffed each attempt, saying that he had given his life to God and that the experience had provided a new opportunity to love God and love people, "which is the rule of my life now," he stated confidently. He closed the conversation by inviting Chad and his friends to be his guests at the Oregon game.

Chad hung up the phone hoping he could someday explain to T.J. how the football star's turnaround had already affected him for the better. *I'll talk to him when I pay for the windshield,* he thought.

Chad stretched out on his bed and took several deep breaths. He wondered how difficult it was going to be to find the tiny freshman girl on campus Monday.

Thought Questions

1. Why does loving God cause us to love others?

2. List or think of specific actions or attitudes in your own life that are not loving towards others.

3. Select at least one of those actions or attitudes and begin working on changing it today.

A Case of Love and Run

"Be careful not to do your 'acts of righteousness' before men, to be seen by them. If you do, you will have no reward from your Father in heaven." Matthew 6:1

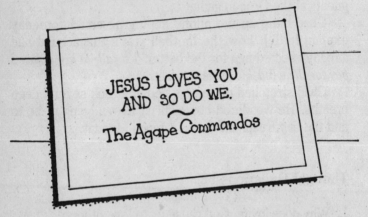

JESUS LOVES YOU
AND SO DO WE.
The Agape Commandos

It was almost 2 A.M. when a small, unmarked delivery van turned off of Main Street onto Thirty-Second Avenue and slowed to 10 miles per hour. After traveling two blocks through a tract of older, wood-frame houses, the van's engine and lights were turned off and it coasted to the curb just before Thirty-Second intersected Forest Street. The streets were deserted in every direction and the darkened houses and parked cars were as lifeless as tombstones.

The side door of the van quietly slid open and eight youthful, darkly clad figures stepped out. The van driver handed out some equipment—two portable spray tanks which were quickly strapped to the backs of the two tallest youths, and six large buckets, stuffed with assorted supplies, for the remaining members.

When the equipment was dispersed, the group leaned toward the driver standing in the open doorway. "You need to be back here in 20 minutes," he whispered. "I'll signal you if somebody's headed your way." The group nodded as they each stretched a free hand to grasp the driver's extended right fist in a collective salute. "Praise the Lord," they whispered in unison. Then they swiftly and silently peeled away from the van and began sneaking single file down Forest Street, being careful to move in the shadows of the trees, bushes, and parked cars. The driver inched the door closed and returned to the driver's seat. He held a walkie-talkie close to his mouth.

The group crept along the sleeping street until the leader signalled "stop" and then pointed to a car parked in the driveway next to a house in the middle of the block. It was a once-luxurious 1969 Cadillac Coupe de Ville which, even in the dismal light, showed the dirt and disrepair of years of neglect. Two of the wheel covers were missing, a side view mirror dangled limply from its loosened screws, and one taillight lens had been broken out.

At the leader's signal the team of youths sprang into action with soundless precision. Two girl members slipped inside the car—one in the front seat and one in the back—and began scrubbing the upholstery and washing the windows and trim. One of the boys with a sprayer began showering the hood with a fine mist, while two others followed him with soapy sponges, vigorously washing the exterior. The washers were followed by the other sprayer who rinsed the soapy water off. Two more workers followed with dry towels, soaking up most of the water before it reached the driveway.

In five minutes they had completed a thorough wash

and dry. Then the sprayers began scrubbing thousands of miles of road grime off the whitewalls with steel wool soap pads while the rest of the outdoor team methodically applied liquid car wax from the front to the rear. One boy unscrewed the chrome frame from around the broken taillight and replaced the shattered lens with a new one from his bucket.

Another team member was just beginning to repair the side view mirror when a sudden whispered warning from the driver sounded in the group leader's earphone: "Mayday! Mayday! Car coming!" One quick finger-snap from the leader and the team members took cover. The girls inside the car hit the floor and the team outside secreted themselves and their equipment in the nearest shadows, leaving the Cadillac filmy with wax in a damp driveway.

Within seconds a blue and white patrol car eased around the corner and cruised slowly down Forest Street. The silhouette of a lone officer in the car did not offer even a glance toward the Cadillac, but continued slowly to the end of the block. As the patrol car turned onto Thirty-First Avenue, the team quickly returned to their task. They hand-buffed the wax job to a silky luster, repaired the side mirror, and carefully squeezed two matching wheel covers onto the vacant wheel rims.

At another finger-snap, the crew gathered their equipment and headed back to the van. The group leader pulled a small red card from his shirt pocket, mounted it on the dashboard in front of the speedometer, and then stealthily followed his group back to the van. The van pulled away from the curb unnoticed, and disappeared into the night.

Miss Frieda Bunson's morning schedule was as predictable as the algebraic equations and geometric theorems she had been teaching at East Bingham High School for 26 years. She arose every morning sharply at 6:00, fed her three cats at 6:15, and stepped out the front door to retrieve her morning edition of the *Seaton County Register* at 6:20. It took her exactly 20 minutes to devour the *Register's* contents along with two cups of herb tea and a slice of rye toast.

By 7:10 Miss Bunson had donned one of her five out-dated polyester suits and had ratted and sprayed her brilliant red hair into an oversized bouffant do. When completely dressed, the tall and figureless mathematics teacher resembled a giant, flaming matchstick garbed for a costume party. Sadly, her personality was as out-of-sync with her students as was her wardrobe. She was tolerated as a hand-crank adding machine in a world of computers and calculators. Over the years Miss Bunson had learned to live with the prevailing tolerance.

By 7:15 Miss Bunson's breakfast dishes were piled in the sink on top of several day's worth of dirty plates and cups, and the morning *Register* was spread carelessly in sections across the kitchen counter. The spinster's neighbors could set their clocks by the roar of her old Cadillac's engine as she left for school at 7:20.

But on this Friday morning, Miss Bunson's schedule was derailed at exactly 6:21. She had just picked up the *Register* from the porch and was turning toward the front door when she glanced at the gleaming vehicle in her driveway. "Awk!" she shrieked, sounding like a cat which had been sat on. "Awk! Awk!" she continued as she clambered down the porch stairs in her faded flannel robe to inspect the sight.

At first she thought that her old Caddie had been stolen and that a neighbor had parked a similar—though much newer—car in her driveway by mistake. But soon she realized that the shiny red and white Coupe de Ville, which had been dull maroon and beige through the 10 years she had owned it, was really hers. She slowly circled

the car several times, carressing the sparkling finish and
greeting the discovery of wheel covers, taillight, and mirror with a gasping, "Oh my gracious goodness!"

When the initial shock began to wear off, Miss Bunson
was suddenly incensed that her car had been tampered
with. But her anger quickly melted. She was aware that,
for some reason, she had been the recipient of an unusual
act of kindness. She had grown to expect unpleasantries
and even insults from her students and co-workers, but
could not remember an occasion of such kindness in her
life.

She slid behind the steering wheel to inspect the
immaculate interior and spied the red card propped on the
dashboard. She leaned close to read the printed inscrip-
tion:

*JESUS LOVES YOU AND SO DO WE. The Agape Com-
mandos.*

She held back her disbelieving tears until she reen-
tered the house.

The mysterious kind deeds and distinctive red calling
cards of the Agape Commandos had been a topic of fasci-
nation and discussion in East Bingham for nearly three
months before the 1969 Cadillac incident. Frieda Bunson
had carefully read each article in the *Register*—written by
senior editor Jacob Smiley himself—describing a number
of "love and run attacks" (as Mr. Smiley termed them) in
the community.

The first such "attack" was reported by the Reverend
Smallwood of East Bingham's Presbyterian Church. It
seems that Reverend Smallwood arrived at his parish one
Sunday morning to find the church grounds looking unusually attractive, especially since the church trustees did little more than shovel snow off the walkway in the winter so
the tithers could enter the sanctuary. Upon closer inspec-

tion, Reverend Smallwood discovered that the flower beds had been weeded, cultivated, and planted in colorful, blooming primrose. The bushes were stripped of their dead leaves, the hedges were neatly trimmed, and the walkways were swept clean. Stuck in the front door of the church was a red business card which read, *JESUS LOVES YOU AND SO DO WE*. It was signed, *The Agape Commandos*.

"I couldn't believe it!" the Reverend had exclaimed to Mr. Smiley during an interview. "When I left the church on Saturday night the place looked normal—overrun with weeds and unkempt. On Sunday morning it looked like the Garden of Eden."

A week later a poor widow in town answered her doorbell to find four sacks of groceries on her doorstep with a red card nestled in a protruding stalk of celery. In the following weeks the local rescue mission discovered their supply closet freshly stocked with usable clothing ready for distribution to the needy and an unemployed resident found his gas tank mysteriously filled with gasoline. In each case a red calling card identified the Agape Commandos as the Good Samaritans.

Even Jake Smiley became a "victim" a week prior to Miss Bunson's ecstatic discovery. Jake, a round and balding bachelor in his late 50s, was barbecuing a hamburger patty on his patio hibachi. He stepped into the house to answer the telephone—a rather curious inquiry, Jake thought, about one of his recent articles. After dismissing the caller rather abruptly for fear that his hamburger had turned to charcoal, Jake returned to the patio to find his patty replaced by a two-inch T-bone steak, ready to turn. On the picnic table beside the hibachi was a giant baked potato, wrapped in tin foil, and a huge mound of fresh green salad in his plate. Neatly tucked in Jake's napkin was the Agape Commandos' card.

"Do you have any idea who these commandos are, Mr. Smiley?" Frieda Bunson asked the editor as she refilled his cup with herb tea. Jake had just concluded a Saturday morning interview with Miss Bunson, another in a growing list of "victims" of the community benefactors. But the school teacher had been unable to give him any more information than the other grateful targets of the commando raids.

"All I know is what I have learned from you and the other victims, Miss Bunson," Jake answered after a cautious sip of the steaming beverage. "Whoever they are, they work with precision and thorough planning. They always seem to know what their victims need and how to supply that need without being detected." Miss Bunson hummed loudly to assure the newspaperman of her attentiveness. "It's a religious group of some kind, owing to the use of the Lord's name on the card." As a closet atheist, Jake felt he had more than accommodated Miss Bunson's proper upbringing by referring to Jesus as "the Lord."

"But why do they call themselves the . . . " the school teacher was enthralled with Jacob Smiley's attention and hesitated for fear of embarrassing herself trying to pronounce "agape."

"Ah-gah-pay Commandos," Jake leaped to her rescue with a precise pronunciation he had picked up from his interview with Reverend Smallwood. "They apparently are not interested in recognition or reward, but rather prefer to conduct their charitable acts anonymously. That's what agape means—loving unconditionally without expectation of response or reward."

"That reminds me of one of the sayings of Christ I learned as a child in the Methodist Church," Miss Bunson reminisced. "It was something about giving in secret without letting your right hand know what your left hand is doing." Jake Smiley nodded knowingly as if he was thoroughly acquainted with the concept which Miss Bunson was describing. He always thought the "right hand/left hand" adage originated with Benjamin Franklin. He quoted the saying to himself annually when cutting corners on his income tax return figures.

"But if we *could* find out who they are and express our gratitude," Miss Bunson continued excitedly, "would such an act foil their secrecy?"

Jake was intrigued with the school teacher's twinkle of investigative spunk. He wondered why, in such a small community, he had never met this refreshing young lady before. "How could it," Jake responded, reflecting her enthusiasm, "especially if the Agape Commandos were the victims of an equally anonymous counterattack?"

"We must discover their identity, Mr. Smiley," Miss Bunson giggled. "How can we do that?"

Jake Smiley pulled a red business card from his shirt pocket, looked at it for a few seconds, and then stared out the window. "I wonder how many print shops there are in this county," he thought aloud as the wheels of his analytical mind began to turn.

Late the following Friday night a group of teenagers crowded around a dining room table in an East Bingham house a few miles from where Frieda Bunson lived. "You should have heard Miss Bunson talk in class about her mysterious car wash this week," one girl commented gleefully. "She has a new attitude and the kids in class can't believe how she's changed. I think the love of Jesus has made a direct hit on her!" The group responded with a ripple of "All right!" and "Praise the Lord!"

"I don't know about the rest of you," a 17-year-old boy spoke up, "but this is the most exciting thing that's ever happened in my Christian life." Several of the members smiled and nodded their agreement. "I've been soaking up the gospel for most of my life and getting water-logged because I had no outlet for what I was receiving. It feels so great just to give it away."

"I joined the commandos for another reason," a muscular 16-year-old interjected with a mischievous grin. "It's good training for my next career—the Green Berets." His friends laughed with him.

The eldest member of the group, the boy who owned the van, spoke next. "We have three projects to discuss tonight and then we need to decide which of the three we will do next." The leader briefly outlined three projects which the group had nominated in previous meetings: replacing the bald tires on the car of the Nazarene pastor, buying and installing a swing set for a neighborhood pre-school, and painting the home of an elderly couple in town who were visiting in another state for a month.

"We're running low on funds," commented one group member who was surveying a small ledger. "We need to increase our dues or do another fund-raiser before we attempt anything very expensive."

"Let's stop and pray about that right now," suggested another member. "Let's ask the Lord which project to attempt and how to finance it." The group spontaneously linked hands in a circle around the table and bowed to pray.

After less than a minute of silent prayer the doorbell rang. The group members looked up and eyed each other curiously. The leader stepped to the front door and opened it. As soon as he saw what was on the front porch he jumped quickly out the door and ran toward the street. The other members hurried to the door to find on the porch two giant, boxed pepperoni pizzas and three liters of icy cold pop. A plain envelope was stuck in the fold of a pizza box. One of the girls picked up the envelope, pulled out a note and read it aloud: "Dear Commandos, We love you too! Keep up the good work! Hope this helps. The Victims." Tucked into the note was a crisp $100 bill.

The group was speechless with astonishment when the leader returned to the porch. "Did you see anything?" one of the commandos asked the leader.

"I got to the curb just in time to see a car turning the corner," the leader informed his rapt listeners. Then he chuckled and shook his head in disbelief. "It looked like a shiny, old, red and white Caddie."

Thought Questions

1. What do you think motivated the "Agape Commandos" in the story?

2. Matthew 6:1-4 records Jesus' teaching about doing good deeds in secret. Read the verses, then list three ways a person might benefit from obeying this teaching.
   a.
   b.
   c.

3. Imagine that you are part of an "Agape Commandos" group in your area. List some good deeds the group could do for specific people in your community.

Lunching with Celeste

"And he said: 'I tell you the truth, unless you change and become like little children, you will never enter the kingdom of heaven." Matthew 18:3

If the juniors at Jefferson Polytechnic High School would have voted for the homeliest girl in the junior class, Celeste Phelps would have easily finished in the top three. Celeste was almost six feet tall and seriously stoop-shouldered, as if perpetually ducking underneath a five feet, eight inch doorway. Her figure was concave where it should have been convex and vice versa. Her straight, mousey brown hair seemed intent on hiding her narrow face, which was splotched with acne pustules and pockmarks.

Celeste's unattractive appearance was exaggerated by an absence of natural grace and an ignorance of proper grooming habits. In short, she looked and smelled bad most of the time. Subsequently, her spirit had been all but crushed from a lifetime of ridicule from her peers. Quietly resigned to her social imprisonment, Celeste Phelps trudged the hallways of Jeff-Poly defensively avoiding those who silently rebuffed her, yet subconsciously yearning for meaningful contact with someone "on the outside."

The junior class did vote on their Winter Festival queen and Wendy McKenna won by a landslide. No one was surprised by her lopsided victory since Wendy always won any contest even slightly related to popularity. Wendy was pixy-like in physical features but her face reflected a mature beauty beyond her 17 years. As a social butterfly deeply involved in student government, clubs, and the campus drama department, Wendy was hardly ever seen alone. She and her large pack of friends kept the junior class in the middle of Jeff-Poly's social whirlwind.

Since they lived on two different and distant social planets, the chances that Celeste Phelps and Wendy Mc-Kenna would become involved with each other were only two. First, it could have happened by accident, as it almost did when Wendy's chemistry teacher randomly paired her with Celeste as a lab partner. But accidents must be prevented or averted. And so the chemistry teacher's assistant—one of Wendy's many friends—saw the mismatch in the roll book before the lab partner assignments were announced. Fearing for Wendy's social status, the friend rearranged the assignments, providing Wendy and Celeste lab partners suitable for their strata.

The two opposites might have been thrown together accidently while walking the same route to Jeff-Poly each day from adjacent neighborhoods. But Wendy's parents presented her with a Toyota for her sixteenth birthday. Wendy only saw Celeste occasionally driving to and from school on Transit Avenue.

Since the girls were apparently not going to meet by accident, the only other possibility for involvement was by an act of God. Had Wendy ever thought about the two possibilities—which she did not—she would have guessed the second chance to be less likely than the first. Yes, God was active in Wendy's life and she had a concern to touch the lives of those around her for Christ. But Celeste was not around her; indeed Celeste was nowhere near her. *God has placed me in the middle of a mission field of junior class leaders and socialites,* Wendy might have surmised. *Why go to a foreign mission field when the home missions front is so needy?* To Wendy, Celeste Phelps was definitely a cross-cultural missions project.

But God was about to act.

It all began in the cafeteria during lunch a few days after Wendy was overwhelmingly voted Winter Festival Queen from the junior class. Her classmates buzzed around her table noisily like drones around a queen bee. "I'm having a party at my house Friday night," Wendy announced above the clatter of utensils and the chatter of exuberant voices. A cheer of anticipation rippled around the table. "And everyone who voted for me is invited."

"That's most of the junior class," someone bragged loudly. "I hope you have a kitchen full of food." Most of the boys in the group growled their agreement.

"That's where I need your help," Wendy grinned. "I'm providing the hamburgers, but you're providing everything else." Wendy's friends overacted their mock displeasure as she began passing out slips of paper assigning soft drinks, chips and dips, and cupcakes to her intimate circle.

Sitting alone and unseen at a nearby table was Celeste Phelps, hunched over a brown paper sack nibbling on an egg salad sandwich. Though light years away from being a part of the crowd, Celeste purposely sat as close to her esteemed classmates as she dared, as if warming herself at a fire while being careful not to get burned.

Celeste listened with heart-pounding interest to the conversation about the party, but remained at her table until the end of the lunch hour when the crowd at Wendy's table had thinned to only a few. Then she wadded her lunch sack, rose, and shuffled toward Wendy's table.

"Excuse me, Wendy," Celeste began nervously, fumbling with the brown paper ball in her hands. Generally quite sure of herself, Wendy was stunned to see Celeste towering over her. "I voted for you too. What should I bring to the party?" She was unable to look Wendy in the eye but stared at the table from behind a veil of stringy brown hair.

Wendy exchanged flitting, uncertain glances with her two friends at the table, then finally looked up at the large girl before them. "Aah," she hummed as she framed her words carefully, "we don't really need anything else, Celeste. My friends—I mean the rest of the group—have taken all the assignments." Wendy hoped Celeste would be sufficiently discouraged to drop her interest in the party.

"I can make cupcakes," Celeste advanced courageously.

Wendy saw an exit from the unpleasant confrontation and took it. "Cupcakes would be fine," she said, looking at her friends for support.

"You can never have too many cupcakes with this crowd," another girl at the table joked loudly.

Wendy scribbled "cupcakes" on a piece of scrap paper and stretched it upward to Celeste. The homely girl accepted the paper as if it were a hundred dollar bill and a rare smile of pleasure brightened her usually clouded face. "Thank you, Wendy," she said. "I make good cupcakes. Thank you for inviting us."

As Celeste walked away, Wendy's friends' faces mirrored shock and disgust at the prospect of their party being invaded by Celeste Phelps. As unpleasant as the prospect seemed to her, Wendy almost felt like defending her ill-fitting classmate. "Maybe her mother won't let her come," Wendy said awkwardly as she and her friends left the cafeteria.

Celeste was one of the first to arrive at Wendy's party Friday night. She was dressed in a mismatched skirt and blouse combination and carried a platter of decorated cupcakes which looked fresh from a bakery. "I took a cake decorating class once," Celeste said proudly. Wendy offered a strained but enthusiastic compliment on the cupcakes and Celeste beamed a broad smile which actually prettied her plain-looking face.

Wendy was spared the ordeal of clumsy small talk with Celeste as wave after wave of her friends poured through the front door. The popular young hostess was kept busy greeting her fans and arranging food on the table.

Celeste stood in a corner near the table receiving about as much recognition as a piece of furniture while the festive crowd swarmed around the refreshments. When someone took a cupcake from her platter she would timidly recite, "I took a cake decorating class once and I baked these myself. Wendy really likes them." Most of those she addressed forced a weak smile in response and then secretly ditched Celeste's cupcakes, judging them unfit for human consumption.

Whenever Wendy saw Celeste through the crowd, the tall girl was in the same place; near enough to the table to tell anyone about her designer cupcakes—which mysteriously kept returning to the platter—but as far from being part of the crowd as in the cafeteria. Wendy began to feel a prickly pain inside which reminded her of the third grade when she was almost always the last child chosen for the kickball team because of her smallness.

Celeste left the party early, but made a point to thank Wendy for inviting her. Wendy honestly believed that Celeste had a good time, in spite of the neglect she obviously suffered. *I guess being ignored at a party is more fun than being ignored at school,* she thought.

That night as she lay wide awake in the darkness of her room, Wendy had a tug-of-war with God over Celeste Phelps. It was not so much a prayer as it was an argument; not so much words as feelings and impressions. But Wendy and God were communicating on a controversial topic.

"But I can't get involved with Celeste Phelps, Lord. My friends won't understand."

"You and I understand Celeste's need for friendship. Who else needs to understand?"

"But I believe in friendship evangelism—sharing your Word with my friends."

"I also believe in friendship evangelism. I'm simply saying Celeste needs to be enrolled as one of your friends."

"But she's so dirty and weird!"

"She doesn't look any different to me than you or your other friends."

"So I invited her to the party—isn't that enough?"

"As far as I'm concerned, you can draw the line with Celeste wherever you draw the line with your other friends."

"You mean I should even invite her to our table for lunch?"

"If I were sitting alone and ignored in the cafeteria, would you invite me to your table?"

"Of course I would!"

"Then remember: whatever you do for Celeste Phelps, you do for me."

The discussion continued until Wendy heard her digital watch on the dresser beep 1:00 A.M. Every objection had been countered and every question answered, though not all to Wendy's satisfaction. All that remained was for Wendy to agree that God had brought Celeste Phelps into her life to befriend. It seemed to Wendy to be a giant step.

She slid from her bed, slipped on her robe, and tiptoed quietly from her room to the kitchen. There on the sink was a plate full of Celeste's decorated cupcakes which had been retrieved from various hiding places in the house during clean-up.

"Okay, Lord," Wendy sighed as she picked up a cupcake and peeled away the paper baking cup. "I'll try to be a friend to Celeste. But I don't have to like her cupcakes." She lifted the cupcake to her mouth and took a cautious small bite. To her surprise the cupcake was fresh, moist, and tasty—as good a cupcake as she had ever eaten. "If nothing else," she hummed to herself as she took a bigger bite, "maybe I'll get a good cupcake recipe out of this deal."

Wendy blew her first opportunity at friendship Monday morning when she drove past Celeste who was walking to school. Wendy pretended not to see her and told herself that lunchtime would be a better time to begin this project.

Wendy's group gathered at their usual table in the cafeteria and Celeste sat alone as usual at her customary table nearby. When Wendy glanced at the other table, Celeste did not look any more like Jesus than she had the previous week. But the penetrating memory of Wendy's midnight conversation prompted her to speak.

"Celeste always sits alone for lunch," Wendy said softly to the friends sitting nearest to her, masking her discomfort at bringing up the subject. "Why don't we ask her to sit with us?"

"Are you kidding?" the boy closest to her gasped.

"Invite 'Celeste the Infester' to our table? No way!" Several others immediately chimed in their no votes. Wendy realized that her own reticence to become involved with Celeste was magnified several times in her friends.

It took Wendy nearly two minutes to pump up enough courage for her next move. She no more wanted to eat lunch at Celeste's table than she wanted to walk on hot coals. As she silently rose from her chair, picked up her tray of food, and walked toward Celeste's table, she could hear a hush fall like a blanket over the small company of friends behind her and slowly creep around the cafeteria. Wendy's secret tug-of-war had suddenly gone public.

Celeste didn't notice the silence. She was enthralled as the Winter Festival Queen approached her. "Do you mind if I eat with you?" Wendy asked the tall girl slouched over her sandwich.

"No," Celeste answered immediately, failing to conceal her pleasure. "That would be nice."

As she sat down, Wendy could feel the eyes of her fellow students tracing her moves. A gurgle of cynical laughter caromed from table to table. *They think this is a stunt or a dare,* she admitted to herself. *They really don't understand.*

Wendy tried to block out the feeling of being in a fishbowl in order to set her mind on a conversation with Celeste. After a few mechanical questions like, "How did you like the party?" and "How is school going for you?" Wendy felt her struggling attempt at friendship already wearing thin. Celeste seemed to think everything was "Nice, I guess."

But Wendy did sense that Celeste was genuinely pleased to have the company, and that, in turn, brought her pleasure.

"I see you walking to school each day as I drive down Transit Avenue," Wendy concluded as she stacked the dirty dishes on her tray. "Can I give you a ride tomorrow?"

Celeste was flabbergasted. "Oh yes," she blurted excitedly. "Thank you, Wendy. A ride to school would be very nice."

For the next two months Wendy drove Celeste to and from school each day and ate lunch with her at least three times a week while still maintaining contact with many in her social group. As Celeste became accustomed to the friendship Wendy offered, she opened up like a flower. She began pulling her hair back from her face, revealing the pretty smile which appeared more often. Wendy also thought Celeste was standing a little straighter than before. Wendy reluctantly admitted to herself that she had discovered a little sparkle in Celeste's personality which had been buried under months of neglect.

Some of Wendy's friends saw the beauty that her friendship had produced in Celeste and a few joined the two girls at Celeste's table. "My parents are allowing me to have a party at home next Saturday," Celeste cheerily notified her table group one day at lunch. "They want to meet all my new friends. We're providing the hotdogs and here's what you get to bring." Celeste proudly distributed slips of paper to Wendy, four other girls and two boys around the table. Celeste's new friends smiled secretly to each other as they accepted their assignments.

Then Celeste's face got suddenly serious again. "Do you think it would be okay to invite Phyliss Hacker to the party?" she asked quietly, motioning toward a girl sitting alone at a table by the salad bar. She just transferred here from Arkansas and doesn't have any friends."

The group agreed heartily with Celeste's suggestion. "Maybe Phyliss would like to bring something to the party," Wendy added.

Celeste's eyes sparkled. "How about cupcakes?"

Thought Questions

1. What kinds of achievements or qualities were associated with Wendy's friends in the story you have just read?

2. What kinds of achievements and qualities are considered most important at your school?

3. Read Matthew 18:1-5 and compare it with God's comments to Wendy in the story. What do these two sources tell you about the achievements and qualities that God considers important? List them here and circle one that you will start working on this week.

The Year We Stomped Saint Bartholomew Twice

"You have heard that it was said, 'Love your neighbor and hate your enemy.' But I tell you: Love your enemies and pray for those who persecute you . . . . " Matthew 5:43,44

I had formed a holy hatred for Saint Bartholomew of the Valley long before I played basketball against them. A fierce rivalry had existed between our two schools for decades, especially during the basketball season when Saint Bart and Faith Academy, the two private schools in our eight-school league, were perennial contenders for the league championship.

While I was still a student at Faith Junior Prep, my two older brothers brought home gruesome tales of their midnight raids at Saint Bart the week before each game between the two schools. The 10-foot marble statue of Saint Bartholomew had been painted so many times that it looked more like a circus clown than the revered patron it was sculpted to represent.

The students at Saint Bart (it was an all-boy school, which also contributed to my low esteem of the institution) retaliated in kind and initiated a number of raids themselves. They had enough dignity not to vandalize the statue of Christ which guarded the entrance to Faith Academy, but more than made up for that weakness by breaking into Faith's buildings after dark and leaving mementos of their visits. Once my brother arrived at school to find the floor of the boys' shower room four inches deep in tapioca pudding with hundreds of maraschino cherries forming the letters "SBV" over the clogged drain. I hated Saint Bart for being so gross and so clever.

I also learned to despise Saint Bartholomew because they always seemed to have a better basketball team than we did. Unlike the public schools in our league, both Faith and SBV are able to recruit players from outside the district. But Saint Bart is also a boarding school. So while we were recruiting the best players within driving distance, they were sucking in prep all-stars from cities and states I couldn't even spell. Furthermore, while Faith's recruits were required to exhibit "fervent evangelical devotion and solid moral behavior" (we even had to sign a pledge!), athletes at SBV had no such restrictions. My brothers described with righteous indignity and a little envy scenes of all-night poker parties in the Saint Bart dorm and faculty meetings in the local bar and grill. And at Faith, recruited athletes had to testify of a history of faithful church attendance. But incoming basketball stars at Saint Bart were accepted if they had attended church somewhere at least once in their lives and if they agreed not to use their Muslim names while attending the school.

So every year's version of the Saint Bartholomew Black Knights was an intercontinental collection of fancy dribblers, half-court gunners, and towering slam-dunkers. One year they even brought in a seven-foot, two-inch Masai warrior whose church attendance requirement was met at a roadside chapel en route from the airport to freshman orientation. My older brother, who saw him play once, said he carried a voodoo doll in his basketball trunks. The warrior lasted only half a season though. It seems he once leaped for a rebound close to the backboard and snagged his decorative nose bone in the net, resulting in serious facial lacerations. And my brother doesn't usually joke about stuff like that.

My freshman year of basketball for Faith was marked by moderate success. In my first raid on Saint Bartholomew I smuggled an active beehive into the locker of the freshman captain. He arrived at the game with his face looking like a bag full of marbles and played a lousy game. Furthermore, the coaching staff at Saint Bart dipped to a new low in recruiting that year: four of their twelve players were under six-foot five. One of those four was Binky Bjornstad, the school president's son. He was a five-foot, three-inch guard who was still singing soprano in the school glee club but started every game for the Black Knights' frosh.

In our first encounter, I stole the ball from Binky eight times and our smaller but faster team out-hustled their bean pole front line for a six point victory. But by the second frosh game with Saint Bart, Binky had grown four inches, added 18 pounds, and moved to the baritone section of the glee club. I still outstole him five to four, but their gangly grove of forwards and centers had learned to block shots and to stuff two-handed slammers. They whipped us by 22 points, fanning the long-standing repugnance I held for the disgusting liberal school which flaunted pipe-smoking faculty members and brandished imported seven-foot varsity centers.

The next two years I played junior varsity for Faith and our team split the two annual contests with an unusually weak Saint Bart JV squad. Our team boasted a blossoming six-foot, seven-inch center, Slick Dutcher. I was shooting better than ever while Binky Bjornstad was still a better singer than ball handler.

In the last game of my junior season, Saint Bart again nosed us out of the championship on two last-minute free throws by Binky, the singing guard. In the heat of a close finish I overzealously hammered him at the top of the key as he started his drive down the lane. He could no more have hit a shot over Slick than he could hit a high E-flat anymore. But he did drop both ends of the one-and-one to beat us.

I was so mad at Saint Bart, Binky, and myself that I carried out a post-game raid all by myself, sneaking into their locker room and spelling, "NEXT YEAR" with pea-nut butter on the mirror. That night I committed myself to run, pump iron, and play hoops every day in preparation for my one varsity season at Faith. We were going to beat Saint Bartholomew's basketball mill twice or I was going to die trying.

During the eight months between my junior and senior seasons, everything took a back seat to my basketball training. My studies sagged dangerously close to academic disqualification. The only friends I saw were those who played basketball with me—and I even drove some of them away with my aggressive, all-business play. Even my family life suffered. If Mom and Dad wanted to see me, they had to get me into a game on the driveway. Once my dad ejected me from a family game on what I knew was a routine charging foul. When I objected that Mom didn't have her feet planted when I bounced her into the garage door on my way to the basket he took away my car keys. Luckily Mom's dislocated elbow healed nicely.

During those months I was on a crusade; I was preparing for a holy war. The intensity of my contempt for Saint Bart was only matched by my passion for basketball and my desire to uphold the name of Faith Academy and evangelical Christianity before our compromising rivals who were at best only nominal Christians. And when formal basketball practice began in early November, my commitment and emotional fervor sparked our varsity team to life. We were intense. We were totally dedicated. We were so fired up we even got into fights with each other during practice. The coach went crazy as he watched a group of average players melt in the blaze of competitive passion, mold under the discipline and regimen of his training, and temper steel-hard in the pool of commitment to each other and to victory over Saint Bartholomew. Coach may have overreacted a little, however, when he prayed during team devotions one night, "God, help us kick those heathen Saint Bart backsides clear across the state"—only he didn't use the word "backside."

But my enthusiasm had not only stirred up my team, it had also incited the rage of the Saint Bart varsity squad. I began receiving anonymous phone calls and letters from the Black Knight lettermen describing various ways they could hurt my body with a basketball.

The cross-town raids began almost three weeks before our first game with Saint Bart and this time the Black Knights struck first. One Monday morning we found 12 gigantic tombstones transplanted from the local cemetery into our cafeteria. Each tombstone had a placard bearing the name of one of our varsity players. We responded a few nights later by kidnapping Saint Bartholomew himself. The statue was found the following day in a box car almost 200 miles from its empty pedestal. But the county police put a stop to the raids with tight security around both schools. The move was a blow to our momentum, especially since Saint Bartholomew's train ride had served notice that Faith would not take an enemy attack lying down. So we poured our concentration and ingenuity into preparation for the game. Every afternoon we drilled until we dropped—picks, screens, fast breaks, alley oops, passing, stealing. We especially worked on Saint Bart's specialty: aggressive body checking. We knew we could outplay them if we could out muscle them.

About two weeks before the season-opening game in our own gym we heard some shocking news. The Black Knights had picked up two transfer students from schools in other parts of the country. The word spread around the campus like electric current: the two new SBV players were trained killers—roundball assassins shipped in as hit men to squash the Faith Academy rebellion.

Saint Bart found massive Fremont Suggs (also known as Abdul something-or-other) in Tennessee. Suggs stood six-feet, eleven-inches and weighed 290 pounds. Rumor had it that "Fre the Tree" could straddle the key, could palm the ball like it was a grapefruit, and had an arm span of 12 feet. He couldn't jump or run, the scouting report said. But he could stand flat-footed under the basket and drape his hand over the rim, and he took only six giant strides to travel from baseline to baseline. The other new player was named Vito "The Mosquito" Bandini, a hairy little point guard from near Chicago. Though he stood only five-foot eight, he reportedly guarded on defense like two six-footers and could hit his high-arching jumpshot from anywhere in the front court. As if Vito's statistics weren't sobering enough, we also heard that he was a member of one of those midwestern underworld families. Anyone who put too much heat on The Mosquito during the game, the rumor informed, would have to deal with other members of the Bandini family after the game.

In a previous year, news about the addition of Suggs

and Bandini to the Saint Bart roster would have demoral-ized our teams beyond hope. But this year was different. We were good. We were tough. We were ready to face the NBA all-stars. We were going to stomp Saint Bartholo-mew on our court and then we were going to stomp them on theirs.

The Black Knights were already warming up when I led the Fighting Crusaders onto the floor to the rabid screams of our hometown fans. There was Fremont Suggs—thighs as big around as telephone poles, arms swatting down practice shots like a huge windmill, and mouth wrenched into a perpetual snarl which revealed the absence of his two front teeth. And there was Vito the Mosquito—buzzing through his warm-up drills and can-ning jumpers from everywhere except the scorer's table. I caught myself gazing into the stands looking for somber-faced men concealing sub-machine guns.

That first game was the kind of bruising battle which everyone had expected. The game must have set a record for most elbows thrown, teeth loosened, and floor burns sustained. It was vicious, ruthless, and beautiful. The crowd welcomed every skirmish with frenzied cheering. The refs tried to keep a lid on the pushing and punching, but they only had four eyes and we had 20 flailing elbows and 100 poking fingers. The lead changed hands repeat-edly in the first half with neither team rising above a three point advantage.

Fre the Tree was formidable for Saint Bart, but he was short-tempered and blatant. He banged and slugged his way into four fouls before the third quarter was half over. Our brave center, Slick Dutcher, who looked like a folded straw next to The Tree's hulking mass, bumped and badg-ered the Tennessee giant under the basket, tempting him to foul. Slick swished a hook shot over The Tree's out-stretched arms at the buzzer ending the third quarter and

Fremont Suggs finally lost control. The snarling gorilla slammed a vicious elbow to the top of Slick's head to pick up his fifth foul. The blow was so hard that Slick nearly chomped his tongue in two and blood erupted from his mouth and poured down his chin and neck. But the dedicated center gamely stuffed a towel in his mouth and sunk his free-throw before heading to the infirmary for stitches.

In the fourth quarter The Mosquito and Binky the baritone guard tried to pick up the slack for Saint Bart's benched monster. Their outside shooting was great, but not perfect. Our hustling forwards vacuumed up their near-misses at one end of the floor and deftly penetrated the lane at the other basket for easy lay-ins and slams.

In the last seconds of the game, with Faith leading by eight points, I felt especially reckless. I snatched an outlet pass and dribbed quickly into the front court. I pushed a frustrated Mosquito out of the way and popped a 22 footer at the buzzer. The crowd went crazy with applause. But the Black Knights were livid, especially Fremont Suggs, who slammed the game ball to the floor so hard it exploded. Then he tore it in half and tossed the pieces into the rafters.

Vito Bandini was equally less than gracious. He screamed at me in Italian and made gestures I had never seen before. I was sure Vito's message was best left untranslated. But as a precaution several of us from the team spent the night locked inside the gymnasium, fearing an encounter with the mysterious Bandini family.

Emboldened with boundless confidence, the Faith Crusaders steam-rolled through the remaining first round games, pounding the opposition by an average of 15 points per game. By mid-season we were undefeated and Saint Bart's Black Knights had trounced every opponent since our first encounter.

But the biggest news about Saint Bartholomew of the

Valley that mid-February was not on the sports page but on the religion page. In the same issue which announced the mid-season statistics, the local paper ran a story describing a wave of spiritual awakening which was sweeping the Saint Bartholomew campus. The school was experiencing a revival, they said.

The report was obviously in error because, as we all agreed, the raving liberals at Saint Bart had nothing to revive. They weren't even saved in the first place. An awakening only works for those who are asleep, not for the dead.

The story went on to say that, as a part of their annual Religious Emphasis Week, the school sponsored evening prayer meetings in the chapel—an interesting idea since clearly half the student body didn't believe in God. On the third night of the series, the sparsely attended prayer meeting lasted three hours. The next night, the handful had grown to a crowd and the meeting lasted all night. Classes were cancelled for the next several days as nearly all of Saint Bart's 455 students crowded the chapel for what the newspaper described as, "fervent prayer, genuine contrition, and penitence in a spirit of humility and brotherhood." Subsequent issues told how the school's regular activities were resumed but with "a pervading atmosphere of concern for spiritual virtues and religious life."

At a varsity team meeting we decided that the so-called "spiritual awakening" was no more than a clever ploy. The Black Knights were hoping either to distract us from the importance of the upcoming rematch or install an early excuse for the crushing defeat they knew they would suffer. Our theory was confirmed one week before the game when their varsity captain called Slick Dutcher. He told Slick that Saint Bart would not participate in any midnight raids and invited our team to join them for pre-game prayer in the locker room. Slick told him we were on to their tricks and then told him what they could do with their sneaky tactics.

The night of the big game vibrated with excitement. We yelled ourselves hoarse on the bus ride to SBV, shouting encouragement to each other and whooping our blood-boiling war cries. The crowd in the gym was as wild and frantic as ever during pre-game warm-ups and the Black Knight pep band blared the fight song loudly. As I surveyed the enemy squad I could see no signs of a spiritual awakening, except that mammoth Fremont Suggs was showing his toothless upper gums through a gawky smile instead of a snarl. *The big lug can't keep a secret,* I thought. *The prayer and revival gig is a joke and he knows it.*

As I took my place outside the circle for the tipoff, the Mosquito hovered near. He stuck out his hand and said with a smile, "Have a good game, brother." I was incensed. How dare a future godfather call me his brother! I slapped his hand away but the smile stayed on his face and he didn't say anything to me in Italian.

The first half was highlighted by suffocating defense and cautious shooting for both sides. The Black Knights played us tight and rough, but legal. We landed our elbows and pushed and shoved. They held their ground and took our punishment without being nasty. Even Fremont Suggs, his cavernous mouth framed with that disgusting smile, played it cool and straight. He only committed one foul in the first half.

What the Black Knights withheld in brute force they balanced with finesse. Their plays were well-timed, their passes were crisp, and their shots were conservative. At halftime they only trailed us by five points, even though we had clearly out muscled them on the floor—our game-plan for victory.

"These guys are intimidated by us," Slick announced

proudly in the locker room. "Their revival gag has back-fired. Now they *really* need prayer." We all yelled wildly.

"Keep punching Suggs and try to draw some fouls," the coach encouraged as we headed back to the court. "Let's put that snarl back on his face."

Slick and the forwards went to work on The Tree in the second half. But trying to muscle Fremont Suggs was like trying to push a loaded 18-wheeler by hand. In his enthusiasm, one of our forwards tripped over The Tree's huge foot and flopped painfully to the floor. Suggs grabbed him by the arm and lifted him to his feet, still smiling like Dopey in the Seven Dwarfs. "Nice try," the giant commended, patting him on the rump. He did the same thing to Slick when our center collapsed after an awkward lay-in attempt. And when I dove for a loose ball, raising a string of blisters on my forearms, Binky Bjornstad was there to help me up—help I refused, of course. The more frantically we pushed and shoved, the more gentlemanly they became. It was disgusting to see the competitive edge drain out of such a once-proud team.

With under a minute to go in the game we were ahead by nine points. They had played a great game, but we had played the superb, punishing game we had planned. No Faith team had ever beat a Saint Bart team by more than 10 points. Not only was the victory secure but the scoring record was within reach. Binky missed a shot with 15 seconds left. Slick grabbed the rebound and shot the outlet pass to me. I decided to hold the ball for a few seconds, then drive it down the floor, past Binky, The Mosquito, and The Tree for the basket of infamy.

Ten, nine, eight, seven. I crossed the center line with Vito buzzing wildly around me, arms waving. I held him back with my left hand while dribbling with my right, watching the clock tick down. Six, five, four. Slick set himself to block Suggs in the lane as I bolted past Binky and

The Mosquito toward the basket. Three, two, one. On the last step before my jump I saw The Tree step around Slick's pick and set himself securely in my path, hands raised and smiling broadly. A split second later I slammed into the seven-foot, 300-pound wall of flesh in the lane. The gymnasium did a complete flip and I crunched to the floor at the base of The Tree. The ball rattled in the rim and dropped through the net, landing on my head. I saw stars and I heard bells. Then I heard the buzzer sound and the ref scream, "Offensive charging, no basket!"

I was sure that the few parts of my body which had survived the fall down the mountain would be pulverized by the monster hovering above me or the scores of jubilant Faith fans who were dancing wildly on the court. Presently I realized that the only real pain I felt was in my ankle and it was severe. Instead of finishing the season with a record basket, I finished with a sprain that would probably keep me out of track practice for three weeks.

Fremont Suggs lifted me to my good foot and assisted me to the bench where my teammates took over. "Hope your leg is okay," he said sincerely. Then he smiled his holy smile and added, "Good game, buddy. God bless you."

I was alone in the locker room wrapping my ankle in an elastic bandage when Binky, The Tree and The Mosquito—dressed in street clothes—walked in. They congratulated me on Faith's victory and expressed concern for my swollen ankle. I assured them I would be okay.

Then Vito pulled a sheet of paper from his jacket and handed it to me. "It's a flyer advertising a concert we're hosting at Saint Bart," he informed. "It's a Christian concert so we thought you guys would be interested. Bring the whole team." I faked a warm "thank you," then they wished me well in track and left.

I was sure that what they called a Christian concert

was probably a group of pot-smoking liberals singing anti-government protest songs. And all that kindness jazz was definitely an attempt to psych me out for the dual track meet with Saint Bart in two months.

I wadded the flyer into the shape of a miniature basketball and launched it toward the trash can near the sink. The paper sphere bounced twice on the rim of the can and then fell to the floor.

For the next several days I couldn't get the smiling faces of Fremont Suggs, Vito Bandini, Binky Bjornstad, and the other defeated Black Knights out of my mind. They were sure out of touch with reality. They acted like *they* won.

Thought Questions

1. Describe the kind of relationship with God the student telling this story seems to have.

2. What was his way of treating his "enemies"?

3. What was the "enemies'" way of treating him?

Escape from Denver

Darci Darrow stepped quickly from the gangway of gate D-11 into the forward cabin of the Boeing 727 bound for San Antonio, Texas. She stood behind a line of passengers just inside the plane, glancing nervously over her shoulder at the passageway leading to the airport terminal.

The tall, slender 16-year-old wore a muted pink sweatshirt under a blue denim jacket which was fastened around her narrow waist by the two bottom snaps. Her strawberry blond hair was pulled back in a pony tail which brushed against the upturned collar of her jacket with each turn of her head. The legs of her slightly faded jeans were pulled snugly over a pair of western boots. Draped from a delicate chain around her neck was a small gold cross which glistened against the soft background of her pink sweatshirt. She carried a boarding pass in her left hand and her right hand steadied a beige canvas bag slung over her shoulder.

The flight attendant received Darci's pass with a cheery, "Hi," to which the girl returned a sullen glare. Had the woman asked how she was, Darci probably would have told her to shut up and mind her own business. She couldn't wait to find her seat and hear the jet's door close, shutting Denver, Colorado, out of her life forever.

Darci shifted impatiently behind a businessman laboring to hang his bulging suit bag in the closet. She finally squeezed by him and maneuvered between several other passengers jostling in the center aisle for luggage space in the overhead bins. After a quick glance at the handwritten symbols on her ticket envelope, Darci slid into row 14 and plopped into seat A by the window.

She unzipped her bag and pulled out her portable cassette player and a couple of random tapes from her collection. She quickly loaded a tape, shoved the earphones over her ears, and turned up the volume, drowning the chatter in the confining cabin with a rush of screaming guitars and drums.

Darci didn't want anyone to sit beside her and she didn't want anyone to talk to her. *I'm going home and I'm never going to see him again,* she thought bitterly. Darci searched the faces of the last few passengers to come down the aisle, fearful that somehow he might follow her onto the plane to torment her further.

The last person to board the plane before the huge front door swung shut was a young woman in her mid-20s. Darci saw her emerge from the first-class section and begin to scan the numbers above each row for her seat.

She was neatly dressed in dark blue slacks and a white, lacey blouse, shrouded with a wispy blue crocheted sweater. She carried an overnight case, and a black leather purse was draped over her shoulder. Darci hoped the woman was a smoker and that she would keep walking to the rear of the plane. But instead she identified the seat she had been assigned—14C—and slid into Darci's row and sat down. She pushed her overnight case beneath the seat in front of her and then glanced toward Darci who had secluded herself behind a magazine.

Within minutes Flight 288 to San Antonio had taxied to the end of the runway. The persistent hiss of the cabin air conditioning was swallowed by the powerful whine of the jet engines which hurtled the plane down the runway and lifted it into the sky for its two hour flight to southwest Texas. Both Darci and the young woman sat through the take-off with eyes closed. The pretty teenager was bidding Denver and all its distasteful memories farewell. The young woman in 14C was praying.

"Beautiful day for a flight," the woman in the blue crocheted sweater commented to Darci, who had slipped the earphones off while she changed tapes. The plane was still in its climb out of Denver.

"Yeah, it's pretty out there," Darci answered almost automatically, wishing her resolve not to interact was stronger than her natural gregarious personality.

"Do you live in Denver?" the woman asked as Darci fumbled with her cassette player.

"No, I'm from Wrightwood, just outside San Antonio. I was just visiting in Denver." Darci finally looked at the woman speaking to her from across the empty middle seat. The girl could almost feel the kindness in the woman's voice—and such kindness felt especially good today. Darci's fellow passenger immediately reminded her of the mythical, intimate big sister she'd never had. *She looks like a talker,* Darci admitted to herself. *Maybe a little mindless small talk will help push Denver behind me all the faster.*

"That's funny," the woman giggled, shifting her body in the seat to face Darci. "I live in Denver and I'm going to San Antonio to visit." Darci couldn't help reflecting the young woman's disarming smile. Stuffing the cassette player back into her bag, Darci turned to face the friendly passenger in the aisle seat.

"My name is Beverly Warner," the woman announced. "Really, it's just Bev—that's what everybody calls me." She reached out her hand toward the teenager in jeans.

Darci grabbed the outstretched hand. "I'm Darci Darrow." Her smile was slight but genuine.

"Did you have a nice time in our fair city of Denver? Did you do some skiing? Were you visiting friends?" Bev quizzed.

Suddenly Darci felt trapped. She didn't want to tell *anyone* about her abbreviated visit, let alone a perfect stranger. *If you were my big sister I would tell you everything,* Darci silently rehearsed her childhood fantasies. As big-sister-like as Bev seemed, Darci's response was guarded. "I was visiting. It was okay."

What Darci did not know was that Bev *did* have a little sister with whom intimate secrets were shared. As an experienced big sister, Bev had detected some lonely, painful words which Darci thought she had adequately screened from her reply.

Bev leaned slightly toward the girl in 14A, her compassionate brown eyes embracing her. "You're really glad to be going home, aren't you Darci," Bev said seriously.

Darci hadn't realized how thin and fragile the protective covering stretched over her emotions had become. She felt her throat swell into a ballooning knot which seemed to squeeze tears into her eyes. She didn't want to cry—not here, not now. But she was unable to prevent her mouth from twisting into an involuntary frown. She buried her face in her hands to stifle the sobs which tumbled from deep inside her.

Bev instantly removed her safety belt and slid into the middle seat beside Darci. The young woman placed a comforting arm around the girl's hunched and heaving shoulders. "It's okay, sis," Bev consoled, "you can let it out now. Let it all out." Darci was embarrassed for her untimely breakdown. But she was also grateful for the unexplained tenderness she was receiving from a virtual stranger. The howling drone of the jet engines served to muffle the slight disturbance in row 14. The nearby passengers retreated obliviously into magazines, books, and slumber while Darci cried.

After a few minutes Bev retrieved a handful of tissues from her purse and slipped them into Darci's moistened hands. "I bet you think I'm crazy," Darci said weakly as she wiped her eyes and nose.

"No, you're not crazy," Bev encouraged. "We girls need a good cry every once in awhile, and sometimes it just happens in crazy places." The two of them found enough humor in Bev's statement to enjoy a brief, quiet laugh.

"I suppose you want to know what this is all about," Darci said more seriously, at last turning her puffy, red eyes toward Bev.

"You don't need to tell me anything," Bev assured. "But if there's something you want to talk about, I'm a captive audience—at least for the next 90 minutes."

"I barely know your name but I feel like I've known you all my life," Darci wrinkled her forehead trying to analyze Bev's strategic presence.

"Maybe you feel that way because we're distant relatives." Bev pulled a silver necklace from behind her collar. At the end of Bev's necklace was a shiny silver cross. The girls eyed each other's crosses and smiled knowingly.

As the plane approached cruising altitude, the flight attendants brought a beverage cart down the aisle. Darci and Bev each selected a cup of fruit juice, then Darci sighed deeply and began her story.

"My parents were divorced five years ago. I live with my mother in Wrightwood and my father lives in Denver." Darci paused for a moment to gather courage to continue. "My father owns a computer software company in Denver and he's very well off. Ever since the divorce he has flown my brothers and me to Denver to visit him two or three times each year."

"Your brothers?" Bev interrupted.

"I have three older brothers," Darci continued after a sip of juice. "As they each graduated from high school and started jobs and college they gradually stopped traveling to Denver. At first we all used to go together. Now they have reasons to stay away, so I go by myself."

"Reasons to stay away?" Bev questioned.

"None of us liked going to Denver because our father is a borderline alcoholic. When we were there he would work half a day, come home, and load up on three or four martinis. Then he'd get sentimental and start whining about how inadequate Mom was as a wife and mother and how she ruined our family, which was completely untrue. He also used his money to spite Mom—buying us things she wouldn't let us have. We tolerated him mostly—me more than my brothers because I was so naive. But we knew he was grasping after something he had lost and desperately wanted back. We tried to love him, Bev—we really did. But eventually my oldest brother Rick stopped going, then David, and then Eric. This was my third visit to Denver without my brothers."

A dark cloud passed behind Darci's blue eyes and her head dropped to her chest. "But now I'm never going back to Denver," she whispered angrily. "I never want to see him or talk to him again after what he did."

Darci turned toward the window and stared absently across the sea of haze which washed the southwestern horizon. She had been holding Bev's hand since she stopped crying. Now she pulled her hand away, as if retreating into a private pain too deep to share. Bev sat quietly in the middle seat measuring her empathy and asking God for a way to convey it.

After several minutes Darci turned back and took Bev's hand again. "This was the first time I have been with Dad alone," she continued. "Even after my brothers stopped coming there was always Sonja, Dad's girlfriend. She lived with him then and did everything with us. Two months ago they broke up and for the first time Dad met me at the airport alone.

"He seemed to be drinking more this time than before," Darci's simmering anger toward her father seemed to Bev to be tinged with pity. "He complained about Mom as usual, but then turned his attention to me. 'You were always my favorite, Baby,' he said late one afternoon as we were walking from his condo to the restaurant for dinner." Darci's grip tightened on Bev's hand. "Then he stopped me right there on the sidewalk, wrapped both his arms around me and planted a long, bourbon-flavored kiss right on my mouth." Darci winced as she spoke and tears returned to her eyes. "He pressed himself against me, Bev, but it wasn't right. I pulled away and he laughed like he was playing with me. But I know it wasn't right," her voice trailed off.

Again Darci turned toward the window, still grasping Bev's hand with her right hand and wiping away small tears with her left hand. Several more minutes passed before she was able to speak again.

"Then last night he came into my room after I had gone

to bed," Darci began again slowly as if each word was a giant mountain to be climbed. "He knelt by my bed and began stroking my forehead. He was very drunk and the alcohol and cigarette smoke on his breath was horrible. I was really scared because I didn't know what he was going to do. He said, 'Remember, Baby, how I used to help you fall asleep by rubbing your forehead?' He kept rubbing my forehead and stroking my cheeks and saying all this 'Baby' stuff he used to say when I was a child." Darci paused again and tried to clear her throat which was constricting with emotion.

"Then he said, 'Remember how I would rub ointment on your chest when you had a cold?' He moved his hand down my neck and started to reach inside my gown," Darci was quivering as she spoke. "I shoved his hand away and rolled to the other side of the bed, but he jumped on the bed and grabbed my arm and started to pull me toward him. I screamed, 'Stop it, Daddy, stop it,' and slapped him in the face with my free hand." Darci broke down again and Bev reached a supportive arm around her as another wave of sobbing engulfed her.

As Darci regained her composure, Bev assured her that she did not need to continue. But Darci insisted on finishing her story. "The blow must have startled him because he crawled off the bed and stood up holding his face where I had hit him. He kept saying, 'O my God, O my God.' He left my room and I jumped out of bed and locked the door. I could hear him crying and swearing in his room.

"I could hardly sleep last night. I got up early and packed my things. I snuck out of my room and called a taxi. I was supposed to fly home tomorrow night but I exchanged my ticket for this flight. My father is probably still asleep."

Darci slumped back into her seat and released her grip

on Bev's hand to blow her nose and wipe her eyes. "I hate him for what he's done to my mother," she breathed coldly, "and I hate him for what he's done to me. I wish he were dead."

Bev was thankful for the reappearance of the flight attendants with the lunch cart, giving her time to frame a response to Darci's story. At first the girl refused her lunch tray, but yielded to Bev's encouragement to eat something. Bev added a brief prayer for Darci to the blessing she voiced over their simple lunch.

"I never told you why I am going to San Antonio, did I?" Bev asked as the two girls nibbled on cold cuts and cheese.

"You just said you are visiting someone there," Darci replied, somewhat surprised that Bev had dropped the subject of her ordeal so quickly.

"I travel to San Antonio four times a year to visit my father who is in a state mental hospital." Out of the corner of her eye Bev noted a look of mild surprise spread over Darci's face. "You see, my father also had a lot of problems. He abused me sexually before I even knew what it meant." Bev heard Darci's startled gasp but kept talking. "As I grew older and began to resist he became violent and beat me. One day my mother caught him beating me and he turned on her. He might have killed her, me, and my little sister if the neighbors hadn't heard the screaming and called the police. My mother pressed charges and he was sentenced to a brief jail term. But while in jail, something inside him snapped. He assaulted another prisoner and then a guard. He was transferred to the state hospital where he has been ever since."

"And you go visit him," Darci asked disbelievingly, "after what he did to you?"

"I didn't at first," Bev shook her head. "In fact I felt like you do right now and I literally blocked him out of my life during my teen years. I'm ashamed to say it, but as a teenager I would ask God to bless my mother and sister and then I would ask Him to kill my father. I wished that the hospital would burn to the ground or be swallowed up by an earthquake. I held a bitter hatred against him for many years."

"But something happened to you to make you change," Darci said, suspicious that Bev was telling Darci the story for her benefit.

"It all started one Sunday when I was 20 years old. The pastor preached a sermon about forgiveness, quoting Jesus' words from Luke 6, 'Do not judge, and you will not be judged. Do not condemn, and you will not be condemned. Forgive, and you will be forgiven.' I can still remember the pastor shouting his main point: 'If you unforgivingly hold guilt over the heads of those who wrong you, God is automatically bound to holding your guilt against you.'

"At first I only thought about petty problems I had with some of my friends," Bev continued as Darci leaned close with interest. "Then one night it hit me: I was strangling my father with guilt and strangling myself with unforgiveness. I had to let go of him. I had to forgive him."

"But he was guilty!" Darci protested, feeling the conviction of her own experience added to Bev's. "He deserved any punishment he received."

"Yes, he was guilty of some unspeakable things against us," Bev agreed. "But only God can justly deal with his sin. Unless I forgave my father, God could neither deal with him or with me. My unforgiveness was blocking both of us from God's grace."

Darci sat in stunned silence, picking at her lunch while the truth of Bev's words poured through her soul. "So you forgave him—boom—just like that?" she asked finally.

"Oh no," Bev shook her head, "it didn't happen right

away. For several nights I fell asleep crying, arguing with God that my father was an unforgivable, demonic monster. But God waited patiently for me to wade through my tantrum and then gently impressed me to write a letter to my father—not a drippy, emotional letter of forgiveness, but a newsy note about the family, informing him that everyone was okay. I wrote several simple letters like that before I could begin to tell him that I loved him and that I forgave him for everything. I'm still not completely healed inside, but it *is* getting better!" Darci saw Bev's eyes moisten and sympathetically shared one of her tissues.

"I'll spend most of the day with him tomorrow," Bev concluded, "and he will probably introduce me to some of the men he has been working with."

"Working with?" Darci was puzzled.

"Yes, this is the best news of all," Bev answered with a bright, teary smile. "Last year he accepted Jesus and has been serving as an assistant to the chaplain in the hospital. He's getting better and God is using him to minister to some of the other patients in his ward."

After a long silence, Darci admitted that she didn't see how she could forgive her father. "He's brought so much hurt," she said sadly, and Bev did not dispute her.

"Perhaps you will spend a few nights talking to God about it like I did," the woman encouraged. "But it is important that you decide early to let Him win the argument."

There was another quiet pause as Darci contemplated Bev's strong advice. "Okay, Bev, I guess I'll give Him a chance." Darci spoke tentatively, but with a hidden resolve that sometimes only big sisters can see.

Thought Questions

1. Bev and Darci had both had terrible experiences with their abusive fathers. Both initially responded with anger, bitterness, and unforgiveness. They were *judging* their fathers. Judging involves evaluation (his action is wrong), condemnation (he's a terrible person), and punishment (I'll keep away from him; he'll never see me again). Why do you suppose Jesus said, "Do not judge, or you too will be judged"? (You can find this statement in Luke 7:1.) List reasons why humans should not judge other humans.

2. Have you ever had difficulty forgiving someone? How did you feel while refusing to forgive? If you finally forgave, how did you feel then?

3. Is there someone you need to forgive? Talk to God— even argue with Him if you must—so that He can help you and the other person.

Y
SC   STEWART
S
         A window to eternity

Date Due

Y
SC   STEWART
S
         A window to eternity

DATE DUE	BORROWER'S NAME	ROOM NUMBER
12/20	B. Scrofton	
10/2/16	NORMA SanTacrose	